Weight

of the

Crown

By

Stephanie Jefferson

ISBN: 1480174343
ISBN-13: 9781480174344

Beyond Beyond Books

DEDICATION

Always for my grandchildren—the very best on the planet.
For Claire, the best daughter anyone could ever have.
For my husband—my hero
For everyone who understands the reality of Girl Power!

ACKNOWLEDGMENTS

Big thanks to the critique group that further my bacon addiction and helped me return to the beautiful land of Nubia. I thank my friends and family that continue to support me in my endeavor to bring my warrior tales to life. Special thanks to Makeda Beck, beautiful cover model, Tamona Kelly=Kreidl, who will not rest until she gets the perfect shot, and the talented Donna Casey, cover designer, who once again created the work of art that covers this book.

1

Kandake stood in the field behind the warriors' compound. The dust of earth beaten with many horses' hooves thickened the air. The temperature was pleasant; a cool breeze from the Nile River blew across her sweat-drenched skin. She had time for one more pass at the target before her duties recalled her to the palace.

She tightened the straps and fastenings that held her breastplate in place, adjusted her quiver and bow, and signaled for her horse to come. Strong Shadow cantered toward Kandake. She headed toward her horse at a hard run. Just as he nosed past her, Kandake rose to the balls of her feet, grabbed a fistful of his mane in each hand, and swung up on his back.

Her seat settled on the horse, she kneed more speed out of him and charged her target. In one fluid motion, Kandake pulled an arrow from her quiver as she brought her bow into position. She nocked the arrow to the bowstring, pulled it back and let fly. The arrow buried its head into the leather-covered straw block, halfway down the shaft at dead center.

"That is the way to do it!" Natasen crowed, running toward her from the sideline. "That is my sister, the warrior queen."

"That was very good, Princess," Uncle Dakká said. As Prime Warrior of Nubia, he strove to get Kandake's skills honed to her best. "Next time, I would like you to hit the target a little sooner— advancing on the enemy only works if you do not give him time to react."

Kandake dismounted and handed the reins to the waiting servant. "I wish we had time to try it again. I am sure I can get more height into my vault onto Strong Shadow's back. That would give me more time to shoot."

"We will begin work tomorrow at first light," her uncle said.

Kandake groaned and headed toward the palace.

"Do not complain," Uncle Dakká yelled after her. "It was your idea to remain a warrior even though you will wear the crown. It is my duty to make sure you possess superior skills.

"Uncle is right," Natasen said, joining her. "You have to be at your best."

"I know, but does that mean I have to start at daybreak?"

"What you are complaining about? You get to leave the compound to do other things. Since Great Mother named me the next Prime Warrior, Uncle keeps me here practicing all day. And when I am not practicing, I am studying strategies."

"I would rather study strategy with Uncle Dakká all day than one hour of diplomacy with Aunt Alodia. She packs more history and facts about other kingdoms into one session than there are tablets to read."

They walked through the palace doors and into a flurry of activity. The servants bustled around them carrying trays, platters, and baskets of food toward the portico. Others clutched vessels of beverages. All in preparation for the feast that would soon be served.

"We had better get cleaned and changed. We have to be on the dais soon with Father," Kandake said, seeing how far along the servants were in their preparations. "Commander Pho and his men leave today."

Kandake walked through the great room. Tall, straight walls made of red-brown clay bricks held the ceiling high above her head; the height of one and a half tall men above her reach. Her sandals made a soft shushing sound as she crossed the floor composed of the same hand-made blocks. She stopped in front of the wall engraved with the faces of Nubia's rulers—past and present.

Several months ago the Establishing Ceremony marked her fourteenth birthday, her entrance to womanhood. It was also the day Great Mother had named her as the successor to her father's throne, and one day her likeness would be carved here.

"Father," she whispered, "I can see your strength, the same strength that has been passed to you from all of these great ones. Will the rulers who come after me see strength when they gaze upon my face? I hope so."

She hurried on to her rooms to cleanse her body and dress. Servants assisted, providing a paste that was a mixture of animal and vegetable fats combined with salts and herbs. Kandake scrubbed her skin with this preparation. Then the young women poured vessels of clear water over her to rinse away the morning's grime. After they had dried her skin, the attendants rubbed scented oil over her body until the dark skin gleamed and looked soft and beautiful.

Around her hips, Kandake wrapped a skirt made of fine linen decorated with painted beads. Hidden inside the folds of the skirt, resting in a nest woven of heavy thread, she wore a small dagger; a gift from her brother, Natasen. Outside the skirt, on one hip, rode the knife she always carried. On the other hip dangled a pouch containing her sling and a small supply of stones.

The young women arranged her braids and wrapped the one just behind her right ear with gold wire. A small golden bell hung from its tip, the same type as the bells that circled her ankle telling all of Nubia she would be their next ruler. A double-strand of beads, alternating black and white, was placed around her neck. It hung just below her collarbones and came to rest in a delicate circle just above her bare breasts.

"Thank you," Kandake said, once the servants had completed their ministrations. She walked to her father's rooms.

The furnishings of King Amani's chambers were set up more for study than a place to lounge. Tables, low benches, and baskets lined the walls. These were covered or filled with stacks of clay tablets, rolled hides, and sheets of papyrus. A large map of Nubia hung on one wall. It depicted Nubia's borders and the kingdoms surrounding it. Rays of the afternoon sun poured into the room through tall windows. Richly colored window coverings of long, cured hide had been rolled up tight to let in the afternoon breeze. Unfurled, they would keep out the wind or rain.

Her parents sat on a cushioned bench nearest the wall with the map of the kingdom. King Amani sipped from a shallow bowl while his wife massaged his temples. He grimaced as he swallowed the liquid and then placed a honeyed date into his mouth.

"Father, are you unwell?" Kandake moved to kneel before her father. She searched his face for signs of illness.

"My head aches," he said rolling the fruit around within his mouth. "The Healer assures me this mixture of aloes and myrrh should ease the pain."

"Kandake," her mother said, continuing to massage the king's head. "Your father wishes to speak with you about the men who captured your brother."

"Yes, Father?" She sat back on her haunches.

"What do you think of Commander Pho's man, Shen?"

"He is a strong warrior and is loyal to his Sovereign. Why do you ask?"

"When Commander Pho and his men found their Sovereign's representative had been killed, according to Prince Dakká's report, they believed that Alara and his hunting party were responsible and took them captive. Then, after you had convinced the commander that neither Alara, nor his men, had anything to do with that man's death, Shen was still opposed to your release. Do you see him as a threat to Nubia?"

"No, Father."

"But Shen challenged Pho, knowing the commander could not fight him. And when you fought in Commander Pho's place, he meant to kill you. How is it you do not see him as a threat to this kingdom?"

"Said that way, he is not only a threat, he is a man without honor. But as you have taught me, Father, things are never as simple as they appear. Shen acted under two concerns: the death of the Emissary and loyalty to their Sovereign." Kandake touched the tips of two fingers, each one representing a problem. She held her father's gaze with her own.

"Shen is a warrior—sworn to protect his kingdom and everything it represents. Here is how I see it. They found the Emissary to their Sovereign beaten and killed. In a new land everyone is suspect. Commander Pho had been told about Nubia, its riches and the strength of its warriors. They come across Alara and his party not far from where they found the dead Emissary. Their loss and rage led them to suspect the first available target—Alara." Kandake gazed at her outstretched hand as if the story is unfolded in her palm.

She lifted her other hand and looked toward it. "For a warrior there is little alternative but to capture those believed to be responsible and then wait for instruction from their superiors."

"After the commander realized his mistake, Shen

still opposed your release." King Amani said. "He even sought Pho's position to ensure you and the others were not freed."

"Yes, that is because of the depth of Shen's loyalty. He is unyielding in his duty to protect his kingdom and Sovereign. I would expect our warriors to do the same." Kandake let her hands fall to her sides. "It was not that he wanted to harm Nubia. He felt the need to protect his home." Kandake lifted herself to one knee, crossed her arms over her chest, and bowed her head—saluting as a warrior to her king. "My King, there is no threat in Shen."

"I agree with your interpretation of his actions," King Amani said. "I had to be sure you agreed with Prince Dakká's report. Because of your invitation for an alliance with their kingdom, I am planning to offer Shen the opportunity to stay in Nubia as his Sovereign's emissary. Our relationship with his kingdom will affect Nubia when you are wearing the crown. Do you have any objections?"

"I think it is a good idea." Kandake smiled.

"Then let us go speak to our people and say goodbye to our new friends."

King Amani levered himself from the bench and walked out onto the portico. His deep brown chest was bare to the sun. Fabrics of brown, green, and gold, colors representing the kingdom, wrapped his hips and draped him to just above his knees, displaying strong legs. Queen Sake walked on his left side and Kandake on his right.

King Amani sat upon the throne, a large chair of burnished ebony and decorated with ivory tusks carved with the faces of the rulers of Nubia. Kandake took her place on the dais next to his throne: the seat that would one day be her own.

She looked beyond the kingdom's citizens to the land covered in sweet, green grass and fields of ripening grain. A cool breeze wafted past her. She filled her lungs.

That is the way this kingdom should always smell—the scent of healthy cattle, drifts of smoke with the tang of hot iron.

The citizens gathered at the foot of the dais to hear their king, standing before him like so many trees of ebony, straight and tall. Their skin wore the glow of health—rich and dark. The solid build of each Nubian boasted of enough food in the kingdom and good medicines.

Nubia is powerful because of the wisdom of my father and the bow of Nubian warriors. Kandake nodded her head. *This is how it must always be.* She turned and looked at King Amani. *And when it is my turn to rule, I vow to keep it so.*

The sound of children reached her ears. Looking down, she saw them playing at their parents' feet.

Healthy children—Nubia's true wealth. I vow to keep you safe from any and all who would threaten you. No one will take that away from you as long as I live—not now as a warrior and not later as queen!

She listened to the king as he advised the people of the state of things in the kingdom. Every person's eyes were trained upon King Amani—each face filled with hope. Her father stood to speak.

"Our neighbor and ally, Egypt, has been attacked by Assyria. At Egypt's request, we have sent several contingents of our warriors to aid them. By protecting our neighbor, we protect ourselves."

Kandake watched the reaction of Nubia's citizens. Some mumbled among themselves, others kept their focus fastened upon their king. All appeared to be waiting for King Amani's next words.

"Nubia is strong. We are safe from attack," he proclaimed. "Nubian warriors have sealed our borders. Nothing gets in unless we wish it."

A roar went up from the crowd. Nubians believed in the strength of their warriors. They trusted their ruler.

Kandake paid careful attention as her father delivered his speech. She knew every line, yet she heard him fill each word with the strength of his character. That is what the people listened for and that is what they heard.

Will I be able to inspire our people like this? When I am on the throne, will I give them the encouragement they need? Will I give them this hope for the kingdom's future?

Kandake was not pleased when her grandmother chose her to be the next ruler, but now she understood Great Mother's choice. Kandake's passion for the kingdom was great, but this was not the only reason. Nor was it based on her willingness to protect it; her brothers and sister felt the same.

Great Mother chose me because I will do whatever Nubia needs, no matter how hard the task nor its cost to me. She brought her mind back to her father's words.

"We have made new friends," she heard him say. Commander Pho and his men joined King Amani on the dais. "And now it is time for them to return to their land. They take with them our invitation of alliance to their Sovereign. Commander Pho has generously offered one of his men to remain in Nubia."

The man called Shen stepped forward, separating himself from the others.

"He will help us learn and understand his culture and we will teach him ours."

The crowd erupted again. Kandake searched the faces of her siblings to see the effect her father's speech had on them. Alara's expression was eager and open. Natasen's face bore the look of one who was determined and his eyes glittered bright with anticipation. Tabiry's features were schooled to a careful neutral, a sure sign that she was not pleased.

Now what? Kandake felt her brow pull into a frown. *Can we not have one day without Tabiry's constant disapproval? When will she learn to see what life offers before she decides she does not like it?*

The king continued. Hearing his words and believing that good things could come of this alliance eased the tension in her body. The annoyance she felt with her sister slipped away to be replaced by feelings of expectation and eagerness for the life to come.

When I wear the crown it will be my turn to maintain Nubia's legacy of hope and prosperity. Kandake turned to look first at her father. He beamed at the people. She looked at her sister. Tabiry returned her gaze. The expression that had been neutral changed to a scowl.

2

"Father cannot be serious!" Tabiry spat, entering Kandake's rooms. "Why would he allow that godless, uncultured brute to remain in Nubia?"

"Why would he not?"

"Do not tell me you agree! What possible good could come of it?"

"Our father has ruled this kingdom longer than either of us has lived. I would say he is wise enough to know what he is doing."

"But Shen opposed releasing you and Alara. How could Father have forgotten? What if they really are connected with the bandits that attacked the caravan?"

Tabiry continued to rant and fume.

Kandake allowed her sister to run through her list of complaints about Shen. When the tirade appeared to be at an end, she spoke. "Why are you upset about this, really? You know neither Shen nor any of

Commander Pho's men had anything to do with that attack."

"But they seized Alara and held him until you forced his release."

"An understandable mistake when you take into account the killing of their Sovereign's representative." Kandake studied her sister. "Come on, Tabiry, there is more to it than that. What is the real reason? Why do you want Shen out of the kingdom?"

Tabiry stared at Kandake, arms folded across her chest. She pressed her lips together in a tight seal, preventing the escape of a response.

Kandake waited. She watched her sister squirm beneath the scrutiny.

When it appeared Tabiry could not stand it any longer, she blurted, "He follows me around." Her gestures and pause indicated that this alone should explain everything.

"And…?" Kandake prompted.

"Everywhere I go, when I turn around, there he is watching me."

"Why does that bother you? You have suitors following you all of the time."

"He is not one of my suitors. He is different." Tabiry rearranged the braids in her hair, twisted the bangle at her wrist, and adjusted the strand of carnelian beads hanging around her neck.

Her sister's nervous fluttering brought Kandake's attention into sharp focus. Tabiry had always taken great care in her appearance, but something was different. This was not the self-assured sister she was used to.

Tabiry had always applied the powdered gemstone and kohl to dress her eyes with the flowing strokes of long practice. Today, Kandake saw evidence of the powdered gemstone having been applied and removed several times. Tabiry twisted her braids and fumbled with the drape of her beads. She never did this. What was bothering her? Kandake thought Tabiry was hiding something. She studied her for a bit longer.

"You like Shen." Kandake worked to keep the grin from her face.

"I do not!" her sister protested. "Why would I like someone who is uncultured? And his skin is pale, like bread removed from the oven before its time. His skin is not ebony or even the red-brown of clay."

"You would judge or choose a man by what he looks like, the color of his skin? He did not choose this color, nor can he change it," Kandake scolded. "In Nubia, a person is chosen by their strength or wisdom. Next, you will be telling me he has no cows."

"Well, he does not… and his muscles bulge. How could I like him? We do not even speak the same language."

"So you *have* noticed his strength." Kandake allowed herself a quiet chuckle. The more Tabiry denied it, the more certain Kandake was that she was right.

"I—he…," Tabiry spluttered. "You just tell Father he has to leave with the others. He cannot stay here." She cut the air with her hand, a gesture that signaled the discussion was at an end and there were no other alternatives.

Kandake laughed as her sister stormed out of the room. She was still laughing when Natasen came looking for her.

"What is wrong with Tabiry?" he asked. "I complimented the colors she chose to accent her eyes and mentioned that she was sure to catch the attention of all the young men in the kingdom and she snapped at me like a crocodile out there in the Nile."

Kandake laughed even harder. Tears streamed down her face. She clutched her sides.

"What is so funny?"

"Nothing really, just a sister's joke. It seems Tabiry has finally done something that she disapproves of."

Kandake was still giggling over Tabiry's dilemma when she found her friend, Ezena, fletching arrows in the warriors' compound. She sat on the ground across from her and repositioned the sack of feathers and bowl of adhesive between them.

"You will never guess what just happened," Kandake said, moving half of the arrow shafts within her reach. "Tabiry has finally done it!"

"Done what?" Ezena asked, attaching a feather to the shaft in her hand.

"She came into my rooms all worked up trying to get me to have Father make Shen leave the kingdom."

"Why? Is she still angry about what happened with Alara?"

"No, it is better than that. She wants him to leave Nubia because she likes him!"

15

"Do you mean 'likes' him as in suitor 'likes' him?"

"You should see her. She is fluttering and fretting over how she looks, and at the same time trying to come up with reasons Shen is not right for her." Kandake passed the veined edge of the feather through the adhesive and attached it to a shaft.

"Tabiry admitted she likes him? I will never believe that!"

"Of course she denied it, but the reasons she used to say he is not suitable are ridiculous. First, she said they do not speak the same language. Then she used the color of his skin, of all things. To top it off, she says he has no cows. How would a warrior traveling far from home, and prepared for battle, bring his herd with him?"

Ezena moved the basket with the fletched shafts closer to Kandake so her friend could place the ones she had finished in it. "If she is not interested in him, what difference does it make if Shen has cows or not?"

"That is what I said. Then she told me that his muscles bulge."

"Ah, so Tabiry has noticed Shen's strength."

Kandake and Ezena laughed until both were bending over, faces nearly touching the ground.

"Speaking of warriors, have you spoken to your mother about receiving suitors?" Ezena asked.

"Not yet," Kandake said, instantly sober. "I am not sure how to approach her."

"What do you mean? You just tell her. Is it really that much different being the king's daughter?" Ezena fletched the last shaft.

16

"I do not think so," Kandake said, rubbing her hands on the dusty ground to remove the adhesive smeared on them. "What if she does not like Amhara?"

_3_

Kandake gazed at the view from her mother's window. Nubia stretched out before her. She watched as a young boy passed by driving a small herd of goats. On a knoll to her left, three women sat on a rug talking and laughing; two of them rubbed grain between their hands and the third suckled her baby.

Coming from behind her, Queen Sake's voice instructed the servants on the rotation of supplies within the stores. Kandake heard the click and slide of the engraved clay tablets that held the yearly tallies. She smelled the cured hides her mother wrote on. The queen used these to keep track of where those supplies were kept and how soon they needed to be used. She turned from the window and watched her mother.

Queen Sake instructed a servant to take the freshest frankincense to the Healer for medicinal preparations. Kandake rubbed and stretched the muscles in her back, remembering the grueling hours spent harvesting the precious resin.

I wonder how much frankincense Tabiry uses to make the kohl she layers around her eyes. She is going to need a lot more the way she is using it; putting it on, scrubbing it off, and then putting it back on again. She goes through all of that just because Shen notices her, but she will not admit that she notices him. Kandake smothered a giggle. *What is wrong with that? So she likes him? Shen is an honorable and strong warrior.* That brought her mind back to the warrior she had become interested in and why she had come to her mother's rooms.

"Where has your mind wandered?" Queen Sake said. "I called you three times."

Kandake's mother's voice yanked her from her thoughts. "Nowhere, I was just thinking."

"From the look on your face, I would say you were worrying more than thinking. What has you troubled?"

"I would not say I am troubled. It is that I need to ask you something and I am not sure where to begin." She searched the room as if the answer were hiding behind one of the many baskets or stacks of clay tablets.

"When have you ever had difficulty asking me anything?" Her mother handed the hide she had been studying to her servant and dismissed her.

"This is different. I never thought I would have needed to ask…." Kandake struggled with what words to use next.

How could this be any harder than going into battle? Just say it. She took a deep breath.

"I think I might want to receive suitors." Kandake forced the words out in a quick, explosive exhale.

"What was so difficult about that?" Her mother motioned for her daughter to sit on the bench with her. "You fight attacking bandits, launch a rescue for your brother knowing you could be killed, and you are afraid to ask me about receiving suitors. It is the most natural step for a young woman."

"Yes, but I do not want to receive just anyone. The ones that present themselves to Tabiry are ridiculous. They behave as if she is the only female within the kingdom. They fall all over themselves to do whatever she asks." Thinking about the young men left an unpleasant taste in her mouth.

"Your sister is quite striking."

"She is, but is that all they see? She is moody, demanding, and allows her fears to dictate her choices. Where is the strength in that?" She scuffed her sandaled foot over the stone floor.

"Some men find that attractive."

"I would not want any man that desired me for weakness rather than strength. I want someone that is confident of his own power and respects mine. The one I would choose will be able to partner his abilities with me. He would not fear me or the crown that I will wear."

"And do you have a particular man in mind?" The smile on her mother's face told her it would do no good to deny it.

"Amhara." Kandake felt the smile spread across her face as she spoke his name.

"Ah, the young warrior," her mother said. "I know him. That explains why he would go on such a foolhardy journey to find your brother. Your uncle says that he has great promise. He is two years your senior, not too old. And I believe he is Ezena's cousin."

Kandake watched her mother's face. She could see her determining Amhara's suitability.

"Does he know of your interest in him?"

"I have not said anything, but he did mention that he would present himself if I made known that I was receiving suitors."

"He has asked you?" Queen Sake's question was sharp. Her eyes searched her daughter's face.

"Mother, he has neither said nor done anything inappropriate. He has been careful to never be alone with me."

Kandake waited for her mother's next words. If she thought Amhara had done anything improper, he could be in danger. The least would be that his place among the warriors would be forfeit. At the worst he would be severely beaten. After what felt like an eternity, her mother spoke.

"I will be watching this young warrior." Her eyes continued to search her daughter's. "You are aware that others will present themselves. Protocol requires that you give each an audience."

"Yes, Mother." *I will let them see me, but I doubt that I will see them.*

"I will speak with your father about this. For now, you go talk this over with Great Mother. Tell her of your desire, and do not leave out the part about Ezena's cousin," she said. "Your grandmother chooses who wears the crown; she must also approve your choice for husband. Listen well; it is important how you proceed."

"Yes, Mother." Kandake left her mother's rooms and made her way through the palace to her grandmother. Because she was not in the habit of lying, Kandake trusted that her mother would believe her about Amhara's behavior, but she still worried.

Why did I tell her what he said? Now Mother will be looking for things to be wrong with him. Kandake brooded as she walked.

She was certain that while she talked with her grandmother, her mother would be speaking with the king.

What will Father say?

4

Kandake rounded the corner of the passageway and walked into her grandmother's rooms. The aroma of smoldering frankincense met her at the doorway— the pleasant fragrance she had come to associate with the strong woman within this space. Lengths of fabric dyed in vibrant colors billowed in front of tall windows holding back dust carried on the afternoon breeze.

She knelt just inside the doorway and waited to be acknowledged.

"Precious Child," her grandmother said, setting aside the clay tablet she was studying. "Come sit with me." She patted the large pillow next to her. "I was reading through the history of Nubia's rulers. One day your name will be added to this list. I am sure you will be one of the strongest leaders this kingdom has had."

Kandake sat on the bright malachite-colored cushion. She breathed in the spicy air.

"Tell me, what has given such a young face the knotted look of an old woman?"

"I was speaking with Mother. I told her that I am ready to receive suitors."

Great Mother was silent for what felt like forever. "The strained look on your face—is it because you think your crown will keep young men from presenting themselves?"

"No, it is because I told her I was interested in a particular young man," Kandake said. She picked at a loose string in the rug at her feet.

"She does not like this young man?"

"Yes….No…, I do not know. I think she liked him before I told her what he said."

"What did he say?" Her grandmother turned to face her squarely.

"Amhara did not say anything, really. All he said was that he would wait for me to receive suitors, and when I did, that he would present himself for me to receive or reject."

"I see. It is Amhara, is it?" Her grandmother's eyebrows drew together. "He is a promising young warrior, but..."

"Great Mother, he has done nothing wrong," Kandake pleaded, cutting off her grandmother's words. "He is careful to never be alone with me. He…"

Her grandmother held up a hand.

Kandake stopped talking. For the second time today she found herself waiting for a woman she loved and respected to believe what she had said. Sitting under her grandmother's scrutiny was painful.

Kandake had endured many such examinations by Uncle Dakká.

When Uncle looks at me like that, I know what he is looking for—am I sure about an answer I have given to a strategy question, am I ready to move on to the next skill level on a particular hold or move, but with Great Mother—her eyes search and search—but for what?

Kandake did her best not to squirm while she waited for her grandmother's response. She had told the truth. What was there for her to worry about?

Plenty. She could say that Amhara is not right for me. She could even prevent his presenting himself.

"Kandake, it is vital that no one influence your preference," Great Mother said, at last. "It cannot ever appear that anyone has the power to persuade you— whether it is a decision about a suitor or as simple as your fondness for a meal. A queen must have her own mind. Everyone in the kingdom must have faith that you will choose what is best for Nubia."

"Yes, Great Mother." Kandake relaxed a little. *Does she really think that Amhara or someone else is telling me to choose him?* "I know what I think and I know when others try to make me think something else. I do not think that is likely to happen. Natasen says I am more stubborn than stone. I doubt anyone can influence me like that."

Her grandmother smiled. "Good," she said, accentuating the word with a firm nod of her head. "Now, let us talk about you and suitors. What type of man do you suppose you would be interested in?"

Kandake felt her face heat up at the question. Her mind's eye formed a picture of Amhara.

"Your smile tells me that you are really interested in this young warrior. That may be, but I am sure your mother told you that you must accept the company of all young men who present themselves."

"Why is that? If I am only interested in one man, why must I entertain the others?"

"Unless you are prepared to choose a husband, all unmarried Nubian men are eligible for selection. It must be clear that the man you marry is your choice." She shifted in her seat. "Otherwise it can be seen as being someone else's choice and not your own. It would appear that others are able to influence you or have power to sway the throne.

"When you choose a husband, it must be a man that will be supportive to your power as queen; not one who will try to usurp it."

"Is that why Tabiry has so many suitors, because she will be Protector of the kingdom's wealth?"

"Your sister entertains that number of suitors because she likes the attention and she enjoys the control she can wield over them."

"They do follow her every wish," Kandake said, shaking her head. "Why would she want a man who has no mind other than hers? If she only wants to consider her own thoughts and ideas, why bother choosing a husband? She might as well be alone."

"Your sister is not as confident as you. She makes her decisions based on what frightens her most. She needs someone to remind her how pretty she is, or that she has skills and wisdom; one that will not challenge her decisions." She dusted her hands as if preparing for her next task. "That is enough about Tabiry."

"Let us discuss the suitability of young men in the kingdom," Great Mother said, her voice taking on a businesslike tone. "Because you will wear the crown, there will be many to entertain and you must take the time to see them all."

Great Mother picked up a sheet of papyrus and dipped the brush-tipped reed into the puddle of ink on her palate. She began writing names, making comments about each one.

Kandake groaned as her grandmother continued. She did not like the sound of what lay ahead of her. She listened with half-hearted interest. Her crown grew heavier with every name Great Mother added to her list.

5

Kandake stood on the bank of the great Nile River. Its waters looked cool and inviting. The late morning breeze picked up droplets providing her skin with moist refreshment.

I wish I had the time to plunge right in, but I have a session with Aunt Alodia. She looked at the Nile with longing. *Discussions about diplomacy—nowhere near as refreshing as a long swim.*

"I heard Mother speaking with Father about Amhara," Alara said, coming up behind her. "So, you have begun to think about suitors?"

Kandake spun around to face her brother. "You heard them talking? Please tell me you told them that Amhara has not been improper?"

"They have not asked me about him, but that is not why I came looking for you," Alara said. "A runner from Aksum has come bringing a message that King Zoskales will arrive in Nubia before sunset.

Father asked that I come find you. He wants all of us on the dais when the king of Aksum arrives."

"Why is he coming here?" she asked. "What do you think he wants?"

"I do not know, but Father thinks it has something to do with the southern border and trade or with his sons."

"Trade is one thing, but his sons?" Kandake folded her arms across her chest. "What does Nubia have to do with the princes of Aksum?"

"Father did not say, but King Zoskales is bringing them with him."

Kandake studied the sky, judging the time. "If I get cleaned up now, I will be ready before my lesson with Aunt Alodia." Kandake tried to smother a grin. "Is there any chance I could skip lessons and go straight to Father?"

Alara glanced toward the sun. "Not at all. There is plenty of time for you to dress and have your lesson." Her brother's mouth folded into an impish grin. "Besides, I saw Aunt Alodia laying out the hides and tablets for your lesson. You would not want to miss Auntie's priceless bits of knowledge, would you?"

Kandake swatted at her brother. He dodged the playful blow with ease. They returned to the palace together with Alara teasing her at every step.

Kandake tried her best to focus on her aunt's words. The warm breeze from the open window begged her to come outside. Although studying things like diplomacy and Nubia's history were not subjects that excited her like tracking or sparring, she recognized that without it she could not have rescued Alara from Commander Pho and his men. Those lessons had kept her from making what could have been a fatal mistake for herself and her brother. Because of what she had learned, she was not only able to rescue Alara, but she also brought Nubia the hope of a new alliance that could mean great things.

"It is important that you understand that many cultures outside Nubia do not view women as worthy to rule." Aunt Alodia said. Her aunt turned to the map hanging on the wall Kandake faced. She pointed to several kingdoms beyond their borders. "Nor do they consider women to have the strength to fight in battle."

"Why do these kingdoms prefer to think of women as weak?" Kandake asked, contempt coating her words. "We are not weak."

"It is the way some men prefer to think." Aunt Alodia shook her head. "For these men, it is what they use to make themselves feel strong."

Kandake pushed aside the hides she had been studying. "If a person wants strength, they should do the work to gain it, not hold someone back so they can appear strong. A man with these thoughts is not anyone I would ever choose."

"There are also cultures that see women only as breeders and servants," Aunt Alodia said. She sat on the chair across from Kandake. "Your reign will be challenged by these rulers. You must never back down in their presence." Her eyes sparked. Her brows drew together. "Know who you are, my niece and future queen. Stand your ground."

"How does this fit with diplomacy?" Kandake asked. "As a warrior, the decision is simple. As a Queen…. "

"The balance is a delicate one. Judge what to do by the presentation. There are kingdoms that will assume that Nubia is weak because we are ruled by a woman. This is an insult—to you and to the kingdom as a whole. It must be countered by your strength of will and your wisdom."

"I do not think my will is a problem," Kandake said. "How do I gain the wisdom?"

"Watch the king," her aunt instructed. "Observe how he holds his ground. Does he do it with threat or does he use subtlety? Knowing when to use either of these is the mark of a wise ruler."

Kandake considered the audiences her father held with the citizens of Nubia. *He is always gentle with our people, even when he must be stern.*

She recalled his handling of a particular incident between neighbors and their dispute over grazing land. One had many goats and the other had a few cows. The one with goats argued that she needed the land more because of the size of her herd. The other argued he needed the land because cows have greater value.

King Amani said that they both had need of the land, but because the goat herder had grazed the land longer, it belonged to her. Then, because the cows needed the grass just as much, he ordered the owner of the cows to pay one calf and the land would be shared forever.

Both hoped Father would rule in their favor, but they agreed that his decision was fair.

"I have watched Father deal with our people," Kandake said. "He has been kind and just. I do not know that I have seen a time when he needed to be harsh."

Her aunt smiled. "There was a time before your birth when the king needed to use his strength and warriors to uphold his word." Aunt Alodia rose from her seat and gazed out of the window.

Kandake looked past her to the ripening fields of barley. She listened as her aunt told the story.

"The Pharaoh of Egypt challenged King Amani over the location of the border between Nubia and that kingdom," her aunt began.

Kandake watched tension build in her aunt's body. Her back straightened as if her spine had been replaced with iron, and when she turned, her face was a tight mask.

"Pharaoh wanted a parcel of land that was well south of the agreed-upon boundary. This stretch of land was watered by the Nile and was good for planting. It also showed traces of gold." Aunt Alodia folded her arms across her chest. "He declared it Egyptian land and ordered that any Nubians living on the land relocate or be killed as trespassers." Indignation roiled from her.

"King Amani responded with force. He had the Egyptians thrown off Nubian land, secured the kingdom's borders, and promised Pharaoh first-hand knowledge of why the Nubian bow is feared."

Kandake marveled at the strength of her father as she listened. It made her proud to be his daughter. She had heard something of this story, but never the details of what had happened.

"My brother, the king, has great wisdom," Aunt Alodia said. "Toward his people, his hand is gentle and his heart is kind, but should Nubia have the need—his arm is strong."

Kandake nodded.

"A warrior focuses on developing strength," her aunt continued. "They build iron into their will as well as their arm. The wise ruler must do the same. They differ in one thing. The warrior is sent into battle to use this iron. The ruler does the sending, placing iron in each decision and command."

Aunt Alodia caught Kandake's gaze with her own. "Be wise, my future queen. Nubia has great strength. Know when to wield it."

Her aunt leaned forward. "King Zoskales comes calling. Aksum has a ruler that does not agree with Nubian ideas about women. Listen carefully; this makes him a threat to Nubia."

_6_

Kandake stood on the dais with her father in the
late afternoon. She was dressed in a garment of heavy
linen. Embroidered scenes of Nubians tending their
herds circled round its hem. Cords of gold braid held
her sling pouch on one hip and tied her knife to the
other. Bangles of ivory danced on her left wrist. A
circle of gold studded with stones of polished lapis
dangled above her right hand. Each item she wore was
carefully chosen to depict Nubia's prosperity and her
intention to keep it so during her reign.

King Zoskales stood at the base of the dais
awaiting formal introduction and an invitation to join
the royal family of Nubia. The sons of King Zoskales,
Gadarat and Beygat, stood on either side of him.
Several Aksumite warriors arranged themselves in
protective positions around the king and his sons.

As the gathered citizens of Nubia quieted, King
Amani arose to address them. "Great people of

Nubia," he said, his voice strong, projecting to the very back of the crowd. "Our neighbor to the South comes to visit." He walked to the edge of the platform. "Come, sit with us."

Gadarat and his brother followed their father onto the dais. They exchanged ceremonial pleasantries while servants set out tables, chairs, and a formal meal. Gadarat initiated a conversation with Kandake. He wore his hair cropped short to accentuate his handsome face of dark eyes and full lips. His ample height matched hers and his wide shoulders gave him the look of a warrior. Upon close examination, she could see that his muscles had seen little work. As King Zoskales' oldest son, he would inherit his father's throne.

"I see that the royal bells ring your ankle and a circlet of gold and lapis adorns your wrist," he said. "So it is true. Nubia will be ruled by a woman." His smile at Kandake was broad and meant to be disarming, but his eyes sparked with challenge.

Kandake met his gaze with a challenge of her own. *He smells of the oil of flowers, not the scent of a man used to labor.* She made sure her distaste for him did not show on her face.

"I find it interesting that your father would not choose one of his sons to follow him."

Arrogant pig! Who Nubia chooses as ruler has nothing to do with you. She gave him a tight smile.

Servants placed the last platter on the table and removed themselves. Once King Amani was seated, Kandake took the seat to his right, indicating her position as crown heir. Prince Gadarat should have taken the seat to his father's right; instead, he sat directly across from her.

Conversation and laughter filled the air from her table and from the Nubians seated below the dais. The talk around her was light. Tabiry seemed to be in her glory, enjoying the attention of Prince Beygat. Natasen and Uncle Dakká laughed with Alara. Kandake even heard her father joking with King Zoskales. The people around her appeared to be enjoying their meal. Everyone except her.

Prince Gadarat seemed intent on talking to her. He talked about his travels and the places he hoped to go. He talked about the women of Aksum. He talked about medicines. He talked.

Will you never shut up! Please, eat your food. If you do not want to eat, talk to Aunt Alodia. She is sitting right next to you. Just stop talking to me. Kandake forced her face to a pleasant expression.

She did her best to focus on what she was eating, but her appetite was waning fast. Kandake looked around for a reason to leave the table, but found none—at least none that would not offend.

Prince Gadarat grinned as if he expected Kandake to be pleased with the attention he paid her. King Amani leaned over to whisper into her ear. When his arm brushed hers, his bare skin felt hot. It could not be the heat of the sun; it was late afternoon and the portico was covered. *Father, your skin is so hot, are you ill?*

"Princess, we will meet with King Zoskales after the meal. He wishes to discuss our southern border."

Kandake nodded her acknowledgement and made a mental note to ask her father, in private, how he was feeling.

7

In the throne room, Kandake sat at the table with her father. Her Aunt Alodia and Alara stood behind King Amani on his right. Behind him, on his left, were Uncle Dakká and Natasen. King Zoskales sat across from King Amani. His son, Gadarat sat on his right. Two Aksumite guards took a position of protection behind them.

"King Amani," Zoskales began. "We have been good neighbors. Both kingdoms have been strong. Our reigns have not been without challenge, but because of wisdom, we have not been defeated. The relationship we share has been one in which we have both gained. Nubia has done well with trade, as has Aksum...."

Kandake struggled to focus as the visiting king spoke.

If he is here, he must have something important to discuss. I wish he would say it. I can see how Gadarat developed a love of his own voice.

"There can be nothing better than for our kingdoms to maintain such a relationship." King Zoskales sipped his drink. "For such reasons, many kingdoms cement their friendship with some type of formal bond. As I have no daughters, I can only offer you my sons. Gadarat is already taken with your Kandake."

Kandake stared at the man. *What! You cannot be serious. This is why you came to Nubia?*

She turned to look at Aksum's prince. She found him smiling at her. Kandake pressed her lips into a tight seal. It was work keeping her thoughts from riding across her face.

Silence fell on the Nubians seated at the table. Kandake sucked in a breath, parted her lips to speak, but her father's touch stayed her voice.

"It is not the custom in Nubia for a father to choose for his daughters," King Amani said. "A woman decides whom she will wed after she has chosen from among her many suitors."

"I am certain that is the case for ordinary Nubian women," King Zoskales said. "But for one as beautiful as Kandake, more care is required. It is known that one day she will rule this fine kingdom. The choice of husband must be carefully made."

"I was under the impression you wished to discuss our shared border and trade," King Amani said, changing the subject. "Is there a problem I am not aware of?"

"That is what I am discussing. With a union between our children," Zoskales said, looking from Gadarat to Kandake, "that border will forever be protected. And after both of us have gone, maybe the two kingdoms can be made one."

This man is more arrogant than his son. Does he truly believe he can dictate Nubia's future?

"I see," King Amani said. His face appeared calm, but Kandake saw her father's body stiffen with tension. She felt his anger as if it radiated from him. "You have not heard me. Nubian women are wise and strong enough to choose whom they desire for a mate—Princess Kandake even more so." His eyes bored holes into the man sitting across from him. "Out of respect for the Princess and Nubia's relationship with Aksum, I will allow your son to present himself along with the other men for her selection. The choice remains hers alone."

He stood. Kandake stood with him. "We will leave you with Princess Alodia and Prince Dakká to explain our customs and the limits of Nubia's patience."

Father and daughter left the room and walked to his council chambers. Kandake noticed the rigidity with which her father carried himself. She put it down to the affront they had just endured. Once behind the closed door, King Amani slumped into the nearest chair.

"Father!" Kandake dropped to her knees beside him and examined his face.

"I am fine. I just need to rest." He massaged the sides of his head. "It continues to ache as if being pounded with stones."

A servant entered the chambers carrying a pitcher of water.

"You!" Kandake barked, "Run for the healer. Then notify Queen Sake." Rising, she dipped her hands into the pitcher of cool water the servant had brought and stroked her father's head and neck.

The healer burst through the door, carrying his bag of medicines. "My King." He knelt before King Amani. He examined his eyes. He touched his skin. "You must rest." He called for more water to be brought. Into a shallow bowl on the table, he poured measures of frankincense and myrrh. These he mixed with water and crushed aloe into the solution.

Queen Sake entered the room, rushing to her husband's side. The look of worry on her face matched the pain on the king's. "The pain in his head continues," she said to the healer. "And now his skin is hot. You must do something." She took Kandake's place, bathing her husband's head and neck.

"Your pardon, My Queen, I have said to the king that he must rest. This is the only way for the illness to pass. He needs—"

"I have work to do," King Amani interjected. "The people of this kingdom must be cared for, their futures secured."

"Kandake can do that," Queen Sake said, looking to her daughter.

Kandake came and knelt before her father. "Yes, Father. Mother is right." She took his hands. "I have watched you. I can do this."

"What of the war in Egypt? Our borders must be protected," the king protested. "And now King Zoskales. I know that Aksumite is up to something. Who will protect Nubia from that greedy ruler?"

"Rest, Father. Be well. Nubia will be safe with me." Kandake put every ounce of conviction she had into her words. "I will protect her."

Her father searched her face. "You are still young."

Kandake stood, shoulders back. She locked eyes with her father. "I am a woman. I am a warrior. I will be queen. Great Mother sees this within me. I will care for Nubia."

King Amani studied his daughter for some time.

Kandake bore his scrutiny with confidence and pride.

"Princess Kandake," her father said, at last. "I entrust Nubia to you." He removed the symbol of Nubia from his hand, a ring of gold set with a large stone of lapis. He placed it on her finger. "Take good care of the kingdom. It needs your strength."

"I will do this, King Amani, until you are well."

Every person in the room dropped to one knee to honor Princess Kandake as their queen and ruler of Nubia.

_8_

Kandake rolled from her bed before sunrise. She hoped to get in some training time before her new duties began. As she dressed, her day's schedule played through her mind. *Can I really do this? Can I take Father's place now?*

 With determination, she tied her sling pouch to one hip, secured her knife to the other, snatched up her bow and quiver, and made for the warriors' compound. Along the way she passed several servants. Each dropped to one knee.

And so it begins. It appears news travels with great speed among the servants. How long before the entire kingdom knows? She took care to give each person a generous smile and nodded her head in acknowledgement, then hurried on to her training session.

Three buildings comprised the warriors' compound. Two long, low bungalows sat parallel to each other. These housed the warriors and their families. The third structure, perpendicular to the other two, stood taller and larger than the bungalows. The second floor quartered the senior warriors and their families. The first level held the store of weapons and a large, open area for sparring.

"Sister Queen," Natasen called out to her as she entered the training grounds, a substantial parcel of land to the rear of the compound. He dipped a knee and then embraced her. "I sat with Father much of the night. The pain in his head appears to be getting worse."

Kandake nodded. "I know. It troubles me." Her neck and shoulders felt tight with the tension of worry. She beckoned to a servant.

"Uncle Dakká says that Kashta and I are to post shield while you entertain suitors."

"What?" She turned aside and instructed the servant to bring Strong Shadow.

"You know, remain nearby for your protection."

"I know what it means," she said, with mild irritation. "Why are you doing it?"

"For the most part, it is because Gadarat has officially requested to present himself and because now you sit the throne."

"If Gadarat is asking to become one of my suitors, I will consider him only after every desirable Nubian male has paid suit." She let a grin touch her lips. "I never thought I would hope for every eligible male in the kingdom to present himself."

"You do not like him very much, do you?"

"I do not like him at all." She took the horse's reins from the servant, ran her hand over the animal's neck, whispered encouragement, and offered him the treat she had brought. "I am not certain why Gadarat is doing this. Keeping the relationship between Nubia and Aksum is important, but to be in a marriage with him?" Kandake frowned as if she chewed a bitter nut. "Aksum has women that are more to his liking." She swung up onto Strong Shadow's back.

"What kind of women would that be?"

"Weak women with no mind or will!" She touched her heels to the horse's sides with more vigor than she intended. Strong Shadow leapt forward. Kandake pulled an arrow from the quiver hanging at her back, nocked it and sent it flying. It slammed into the target with such force its head protruded from the other side.

I have more important things to worry about than you, Prince Gadarat; I have a kingdom to care for.

When Kandake arrived in her rooms, several servants waited to assist with her bath and dress. She stepped into the cleansing booth. Two young women poured water over her. Two others slathered her skin with a paste of vegetable fat, aloes, and myrrh. They rinsed Kandake's body, dousing her skin with clear water. After the second lather and rinse, Kandake stepped from the bath, toweling herself dry using a cloth of heavy woven cotton. Her grandmother stood looking out of the window.

"Great Mother, I was not expecting you," Kandake said.

"Tradition warrants I dress you the first time you sit the throne," her grandmother said.

"I know, but today I am merely filling in until Father is well. This is not my rule."

"You are sitting the throne. It *is* your rule."

"Father passed the ring to me last night. Is there need for this ceremony?"

Her grandmother held up a hand, stopping Kandake. "When your father is well enough, he will return to the throne, but once you sit, the rule is yours. Therefore, I dress you to meet your people." Great Mother indicated the clothing that lay on her bed. "These are for you."

Kandake lifted the dress. Its fabric had been dyed with vibrant colors of red, green and gold. Each color had the appearance of shifting gradually into the other. Servants lifted it above her head, pulled it down and smoothed it over her body. The straps at her shoulders were as wide as three fingers. Pleating narrowed them to the width of one finger where they attached to the dress. The cotton sheath nestled along each of Kandake's curves.

Servants draped a robe of near transparent linen over her. It was white with pleats running down the center of Kandake's back. She sat for them to place sandals of soft leather on her feet.

Her grandmother held a package of white linen tied by a single, thin gold wire. When Great Mother opened the wire-and-linen wrapping, morning light bounced from the surface of the revealed object. The reflected light mirrored the brilliance of an afternoon sun in Nubia.

"Great Mother," Kandake whispered, in awe of the beauty of her crown. Tradition required that every sitting ruler have his or her own crown. Hers was different from her father's. Many strands of gold braided in an intricate pattern made up the band that would encircle her brow, its height as tall as the length of Kandake's thumb. A large stone of lapis rested where the ends of the band met at the front. The gem nestled between a replica of miniature cow horns carved from ivory. Two golden, hooded cobras appeared to emerge from the stone.

The woven gold of the band designated Kandake as Nubia's ruler and the unification of its people. Cow horns, signifying the kingdom's wealth, embraced the large blue gem. The lapis stone symbolized the kingdom with its blessing from their god. Its deep blue color and spangles of gold flecks represent the heavens and the vipers rising from it spoke of Nubia's strength. It also warned of the Kingdom's deadly warriors. These elements of the royal headdress projected to all the wealth, strength, and unity of the kingdom of Nubia.

Kandake had always thought her father's crown beautiful and knew hers would be, too, but this was more than she had expected.

"Rise, Princess Kandake," Great Mother said with the formality the ritual required. Kandake's uncles, aunt, brothers, sister, and mother entered the room.

Kandake stood. Great Mother placed the crown upon her head. Every person in the room dropped to one knee, bowing before Kandake, Queen of Nubia.

The weight of the crown felt good and right, yet the responsibility it represented added to its heaviness. Kandake looked at the bowed heads of her family and servants. *I will do this well.*

She extended a hand each to her mother and grandmother and lifted them from their knees. "Mother, you have taught me about Nubia and its beauty. Great Mother, you have taught me about myself. I vow to use this knowledge to keep all of Nubia great and strong. I will protect every citizen with all that I am. Every decision I make will be for the good of this kingdom." At her nod, the others rose.

Uncles and aunt embraced Kandake and kissed her forehead.

Natasen stepped in front of her. He dropped again to one knee, crossed his arms over his chest and bowed his head, offering his sister the full salute of a Nubian warrior.

"My sister and My Queen," he said. "I vow to keep your kingdom safe. I will protect it with my life. None shall harm Nubia, or you, My Queen."

"Thank you, Natasen," she said, laying her hand on the back of his head, conferring honor to the warrior before her.

Alara stepped forward next. He took a knee before his sister. "My Queen, I vow to offer you wisdom and good counsel."

She honored him with her hand, as well.

"Little sister, My Queen," Tabiry said, bowing before Kandake. "I vow to protect the kingdom's wealth." She received the Queen's honor, like her brothers.

Kandake's siblings stood. The faces of Alara and Natasen shone. Natasen's smile held love and respect. Alara's displayed pride and dignity. As usual, Tabiry looked straight at Kandake, her face rigid and unreadable.

Kandake stared back. *Now what?*

9

Kandake strode into the throne room to begin her first day of audiences as queen. Alara and Aunt Alodia followed behind. The throne upon which she sat was not her father's. Its size was the same as his and it was made of ebony with ivory carvings of past Nubian rulers. But her throne included King Amani's visage as a past king. The sight of it filled her with great anticipation and sadness.

She stroked his likeness. *Please Father, be well.* With squared shoulders and lifted chin, Kandake began her first session.

She worked long hours listening to the complaints and problems of the citizens of Nubia. After she had met with the last of the citizens presenting themselves for the day, she stood and stretched.

"Prince Alara," she said. "We are finished for the day. What do you think of a long walk with me? I would like to see the land that Nuri is asking for."

"That would be very enjoyable," her brother said. "I will instruct the servants to prepare a meal we can eat along the way." When Alara received the packet of food from the servant, he and Kandake walked outside.

"The sun is kind today—not very hot," Kandake said. She stopped at the edge of the courtyard to the rear of the palace and enjoyed the soft breeze. Not far away, beneath a cluster of trees, several small children played together while their mothers ground grain. The corners of her mouth lifted as the squeals and laughter reached her ears and heart.

A small boy turned his head toward her and left the group. He toddled as he ran straight at Kandake and grabbed her knees in a fierce embrace. "Princess, Princess," he said, leaning his head back to see her face.

Kandake stooped to make eye contact with the child. "Good day," she said. "What is your name?" Food smeared his face and dust from the ground covered his hands and arms. He transferred a good portion of it onto her beautiful dress.

"Oh, no, My Queen," a woman said, running to Kandake. "Please, we ask your pardon." Once she extricated her son, she dropped to one knee and attempted to pull her son down with her.

"There is no need for pardon," Kandake said.

"But your clothing! He has gotten food and dirt all over you." the mother said, apprehension coloring her voice and drawing lines across her brow. She directed sounds of disapproval toward the boy.

Kandake stood. She beckoned the mother to rise. "Children express their joy when they feel it. As he is a citizen of this kingdom, it is my honor to be the object of that delight." Her hand brushed at the stains. "Next time, I will be sure to change into clothing more appropriate for all of Nubia's people." She smiled at the child and chucked him under his chin.

"Thank you, My Queen." The woman beamed at Kandake and took her son back to where she worked.

"It is easy to see the wisdom in Great Mother's choice of ruler," Alara said.

They walked to the tanner's low, open structure. The odor of curing hides greeted them. Nuri sat at a tall table, drawing her blade across a fresh skin. She stood, dusting bits of animal flesh from her arms as Kandake and Alara approached. She dipped a knee.

"I came to talk with you about the land you are requesting," Kandake said, after acknowledging the tanner. "Do you have time to walk with us?"

"Of course, My Queen." They walked behind the structure and down a gentle slope. "I would like to move my work and hides to that area over there," Nuri said. She pointed along the base of the slope.

The place Nuri hoped to obtain was close to a narrow stream that ran shallow from bank to bank. The ground was level but contained too many rocks for adequate cultivation of crops and posed a danger to the hooves of grazing herds. Knots of ebony trees dotted the landscape.

"It is far enough from others that the smell of my work should not bother anyone. This parcel is large enough that I could take on apprentices without being crowded."

"I see," Kandake said. "I will speak with the council, but I do not see any reason your request should be denied."

"Thank you, My Queen."

Kandake and Alara, leaving Nuri to her work, walked to an acacia and sat in the shade the tree provided.

"What is on your mind, My Queen?" Alara asked.

"What I need right now, is to have a conversation with my brother, not my advisor," she said.

"Of course, My Queen. I am here." Alara grinned.

"You call me 'My Queen' one more time and I will hit you."

"Yes, My—"

She gave him a gentle slap on the arm. "I want to know what you think about Gadarat and his desire to present himself."

"I believe he and his father are hoping for a way to get as much Nubian land as they can without starting a war between the two kingdoms."

"That is what I think, too. But would he truly bind himself with marriage to get it? He does not know me well, and if he did, he would not like me. I can tell he has no respect for women nor does he have respect for my ability to rule this kingdom."

"That is why he is attempting to do whatever he must to gain your favor. A marriage between the two of you ties Nubia to Aksum. It is likely he believes this will give him control of this kingdom."

"I would never choose him. There is even less chance that I would allow him to have any power in Nubia." She watched an insect struggling to carry a leaf much greater than itself. "Why must I allow him my company?"

"It is tradition, little sister, and it is because of your position as queen that you must receive all who present themselves."

"That is what Great Mother says. If I could, that is one tradition I would change."

"I think allowing him to become one of your suitors is a good idea. And before you object, let me explain." Alara passed Kandake a small serving of cheese and a portion of meat from the food pouch. "Men like Gadarat believe they are smarter than those around them. This belief is stronger when he is in the company of women, and, because of this, he will be less guarded in what he says. Spending time with him will give you an opportunity to know what his thoughts and plans are."

Kandake sat chewing, listening to her brother, and deep in thought. She lifted the bladder lying at her feet and sipped the cool water from it. "I understand what you are saying. I will do whatever Nubia needs of me, but this is one thing that I will not like. Not at all."

10

Kandake returned to the palace refreshed from her lunch with Alara. She changed her clothing and went to her father's rooms. When she arrived, her mother was sitting on a bench next to his bed, bathing King Amani's brow. The window coverings had been lowered to block the light from the afternoon sun. Someone had cleared the table-tops of the usual stacks of clay tablets and piles of rolled hides. The air in the room felt different. It was missing her father's normal bustle of activity.

"How is he?" Kandake asked, in a whisper as she sat on the bench next to her mother.

"He is resting," Queen Sake said. "The healer just left. He says your father must sleep."

"How can I sleep when the Queen of Nubia pays me a visit?" King Amani croaked, his voice hoarse with pain and fatigue. He turned onto his side to face

Kandake. "I am told that your first audience with our people went well."

"It did, Father," Kandake said, her voice filled with excited confidence. "The most interesting appeal of the day is that Nuri has decided to take on apprentices and has requested to move her workspace to the rocky area over the knoll."

She detailed the session for him and explained her reasons for the decisions she had made. When Kandake finished her recitation of the day, King Amani rolled onto his back. "I am proud of you," he said. He swiped a hand over his face. A slight tremor evident in the hand he used.

"Father, I have tired you. I will go. You need to rest."

"Not before I ask one more question. I understand that Prince Gadarat has formally requested to become one of your suitors. Will you see him?"

"I will, but not for the reason he thinks." Her worry turned to irritation. "He thinks I should be impressed because he can fill a room with words or because his face is pleasant to look at. His manner tells me he believes women are weak and so must think the same of me. I am allowing him to see me to find out what his plans are. I want to know if I need to strengthen that border." Her irritation with the man and his father mounted. "It is his fortune that tradition requires I entertain his request. My choice would be to throw that prince across Strong Shadow's back and dump him back into Aksum."

King Amani's body began to shake. "Father! What is it?" Kandake turned to her mother. "Should we get the healer?"

"Amusement does not require herbs or medicines." Humor and delight colored her mother's words.

❧❧

Kandake found Ezena standing near the bank of the Nile. She appeared to be staring across the water's expanse.

"Are you looking for anything in particular?" Kandake asked, coming to stand next to her friend.

"No, I was thinking about how things will change now that you rule," Ezena said, dropping to one knee.

"What things?" She motioned for her friend to rise.

"Hunting, escorting the caravans, training—things like that."

"Some things do have to change, but not that many. One change is that I will not be able to escort caravans for now, but I am still training. I do that very early in the morning. I can still hunt, but the party will have to include several warriors."

"I know, but it will be different."

"You promised you would still be my friend even if I wear the crown." Kandake touched Ezena's arm. "You cannot stop now. I need a friend more than ever. Who would I talk to?"

"You have Alara," Ezena said. "Aside from that, with all that you have to do, where will you get the time?"

"I will make the time," Kandake said. "I rise early in the morning to continue to train with Uncle Dakká. We could make a practice of eating evening meal together." She worked her face into the expression that always succeeded in getting her brother to agree with her.

"Stop. I will do it, but not because of that pitiful face. It does not work with me. I am not your brother. After all, who will you talk with about Amhara?"

11

Kandake had evening meal laid out in her rooms. Ezena came in as the last dish was set on the table.

"It smells good," Ezena commented as she took her seat. She placed sliced meat, cheese, bread, and a few radishes on her plate. "Is it true Prince Gadarat is planning on presenting himself to you?"

"It is true." Kandake did not try to hide her feelings of dislike for the man.

"Will you accept him?"

"It is unfortunate, but I must treat him the same as I do the others. Tradition says I have to allow him the time, but I am really only interested in one person." Kandake smiled at her friend.

"When will you begin receiving your suitors?"

"I will receive my first one in two days."

"Is not that the time Amhara returns from his hunt?"

Tabiry strode into the room. In measured steps, she tromped to the end of the table and glared at her sister. "Now that you are Queen, I suppose you have the power to do it."

"Power to do what? Whatever it is, I am sure it can wait until after I finish this meal with my friend."

"This is just like you. See to your own needs, never mind about the suffering of others."

"What suffering? Who is suffering?" Kandake set down her drinking bowl. "Neither Aunt Alodia nor Alara have said anything to me about someone suffering. What are you talking about?"

"I am suffering. I asked you to have Father send Shen away and you refused. Now he has decided to present himself as a suitor and I have to accept him. What do you plan to do about it?" Tabiry jammed her fists on her hips. She looked like a goose ready to take flight the way her elbows stuck out at her sides.

Kandake sighed. She worked hard to be patient with her sister. "What is it you want me to do about it?"

"Tell him he cannot present himself. Send him home. I do not care what you do. Just make sure he is not here. I do not want him as a suitor."

"Tabiry, you have to follow our kingdom's traditions, as do I."

"That is good for you. You have the prince of Aksum presenting himself and I am harnessed with this...this warrior of Scythia."

"I would prefer the warrior," Kandake murmured. "Shen is a guest of Nubia, emissary from an allied kingdom. It is his right to present himself if he chooses. Why are you insisting that I do something? You could choose to ignore him like you do all of the rest of your suitors."

Tabiry scowled at Kandake. "I cannot just ignore him. If you will not help me, I will ask Uncle Dakká. He will protect me." She left the room with all of the grace of a charging rhinoceros.

After the door closed behind Tabiry, Kandake and Ezena burst into laughter.

"How do you stand it?" Ezena asked. "If she is not complaining about one thing, it is another. What does it matter if he presents himself? She does not have to choose him."

"I believe that is the problem. Her manner causes me to think it may be that she wants to choose him," Kandake said. "If she takes a husband, many things will change for Tabiry."

"The only thing I see changing is the trail of suitors leading to her door. It does nothing to affect her position as Protector of Nubia's wealth."

"Living without her throng of admirers will not be easy for her," Kandake said, feeling more compassion toward her sister than her laughter implied. "Tabiry's confidence goes only as far as her ability to cause certain men to desire her. These men do whatever she says to gain her approval. Shen is a man no woman controls."

"But Tabiry can do many things," Ezena said, surprise painting itself over her face. "I have witnessed her gentleness with our elders. She enjoys chewing for those without teeth and feeding them. I have seen her leading others who could not walk on their own. For many, she rubs oils into their skin. Who could not see her generous heart?"

Kandake nodded her agreement. "Tabiry is the only one who does not. I am certain it is the reason Great Mother named her as Protector. Tabiry enjoys receiving gifts and trading for whatever she wishes, but she shares most of it with the old mothers." Kandake drank the last of her juice and set the bowl down.

"I set aside some sweetroot to give Strong Shadow. Do you have time to walk with me?" Kandake asked. She pushed away from the table.

Kandake and Ezena left the palace heading in the direction of the stables. Whoever she encountered along the way dipped a respectful knee. She acknowledged their respect with a kind smile.

"How do you become comfortable with people bowing everywhere you go?" Ezena asked.

"I will let you know when it happens. When Great Mother named me as my father's successor, everyone bowed for the first week as tradition requires. That was a very long week. Now, it will occur until the king resumes his throne. He cannot return soon enough."

"How is King Amani? Has his health returned?"

"Not yet. The pain continues in his head and he is asleep more than he is awake." She reached out to her friend. "I am worried."

Kandake walked in silence with Ezena until they reached the stable entrance. She whistled for her horse.

Strong Shadow's answering nicker came from his stall at the end of the corridor. He met her at the rope tied across its opening.

She passed her hand over the horse's muzzle and scratched between his ears, all the while offering reassuring whispers to her equine friend. She fed Strong Shadow the treat she had brought him. "Ezena, you have been keeping company with Nateka for a few weeks, now. Have many others presented themselves?"

"There have been a few, but I am still only interested in him."

The smile on Ezena's face told Kandake everything she could have asked about her friend's growing feelings for Nateka. They left the stables and returned to Kandake's rooms within the palace.

"So when the others come to pay suit, how do you manage their attention?" Kandake asked. They relaxed in the seating area near a window and requested cool water to be brought.

"I am polite and allow them to take me for walks or share a meal. There are some whose company I do enjoy—of course not as much as Nateka's." She accepted the water offered her.

"I will try that. It seems that I will have many more than I would prefer. There are two in particular that I have concern about. With one, I would like to spend as much time as I possibly can. The other could dive into the Nile and never return."

12

A few days later, Kandake rose shortly after sunrise to bathe and dress. She wanted to get an early start, because once she dispensed with the morning's requirements, she would begin her first day of receiving suitors.

Today, Amhara returns from his hunt. Delight colored her thoughts. *This is the afternoon he presents himself.* Excitement ran through her.

This morning, she took special care with how she dressed. She took time to sketch kohl around her eyes in an artful manner. She applied the powder she had ground from malachite to her lids. The color accentuated the length of vibrant fabric she wrapped around her hips.

A servant held up a sheet of polished copper for Kandake to inspect her ministrations in its reflection. *I cannot believe I am spending this much time dressing, painting my eyes, and rearranging my braids. One would think I have been taking lessons from Tabiry.* With a final glance and a soft giggle, she headed off to begin her day.

Kandake worked hard all morning. It was not the business at hand that offered her difficulty. Rather, it was keeping her mind on the day's scheduled matters that caused her trouble.

After hearing the last of the reports and proposals, Kandake left the council chambers and walked at a very brisk pace to the room that had been set aside for her to entertain her suitors. It was smaller than the throne room, but larger than the council chambers. All of the window coverings were rolled up or lashed back to let in the daylight and to allow for observation and supervision.

Cloths with depictions of life in Nubia hung from the walls. Chairs, placed in a conversational arrangement, clustered toward the center of the space. Amidst them, a small table had been set with beverages, an assortment of cheeses and vegetables, and the savory olives Kandake preferred.

Kashta and Natasen reached the room ahead of her. Kandake acknowledged them as she crossed the area and seated herself in one of the arranged chairs. She sipped on a mixture of fruit juices and nibbled cheese waiting for Amhara's arrival.

She did not have to wait long. Amhara came to the doorway and paused for permission to enter. His bare chest glowed with the look of burnished ebony. He had wrapped a tanned hide about his hips. It had been dyed a subdued green, matching the leaves of the acacia tree. Beads dangled where the wrap was tied at his waist. The fabric draped to the middle of his thighs, accentuating the work-hardened muscles.

"Amhara, I am pleased to have you visit," Kandake said, using the traditional greeting. It took work keeping calm in her voice. *Why is my heart racing like this? I have spent many hours sparring with this man. We have hunted together.*

Amhara stepped into the space. He nodded toward the warriors on his way to Kandake.

"Thank you for receiving me. I will not keep you long," he said. His response was formal as he sat in the chair across from her.

"Would you care for refreshment?" Kandake asked, offering him a filled cup. He accepted the beverage and sipped before setting it on the table.

"May I end your hunger?' Amhara took a small dish. In it he placed several slices of cheese, a radish, and a few olives.

Kandake received the dish, ate a slice of cheese and the radish, then set the bowl on the table.

Having completed the required custom and tradition, Kandake waited for Amhara to speak. She toyed with the bracelet on her wrist.

"My Queen, I am a strong warrior," Amhara said. "This year, I will advance from apprentice to journeyman status. It is my desire to become a senior warrior and I am training toward that advancement." He listed his qualities; all of the things he hoped would influence her to consider him. "I have one cow and she is with calf. It is due to be born within a few weeks. I will trade the calf for enough land to build and plant. I would like children, but I am of a mind that those should come after the marriage is strong." Here he took a breath and continued. "I am not quick to temper, nor am I harsh. I am most times gentle, but I must admit that I am ready to cause harm to those who hurt people I love."

Kandake listened. She enjoyed the sound of Amhara's voice. She admired the way he held himself; sitting tall, presenting with strength.

It pleases me that you are here. You are the only one I choose to entertain. I entertain the others because of tradition. I have always respected what I have seen in you. If I were choosing a husband today, I am sure it would be you.

At the end of Amhara's recitation, Kandake offered her plate for him to eat from, indicating her formal acceptance of him as a suitor. Amhara selected a slice of cheese and an olive. He chewed, maintaining eye contact with her. He drained his cup and stood to leave. "It would please me to see you again. Would you walk with me, or maybe share a meal?"

Kandake rose, placed her hands behind her, signifying there were no barriers between them. "I would enjoy that," she said.

Amhara dipped a knee and nodded to the warriors as he left the room.

Kandake watched the lines of the muscles in his back as Amhara walked through the doorway. *I would enjoy it indeed.*

The next two young men to present themselves could have been twins. They each had very little in their manner that was the least bit interesting to

Kandake. On several occasions during their visits, she had to pull her mind away from reviewing her schedule for the days ahead. The third to present himself following Amhara pricked Kandake's heart. His nerves got the better of him. He almost missed the chair when he took his seat. When it came time for him to prepare a dish of food for her, his hands shook so much, it was difficult to keep the olives from rolling off of the plate.

Kandake could not bring herself to offer him the food he had prepared for her, but neither could she turn him away altogether. When he stood to leave, she folded her hands in front of her, giving him the opportunity to present himself again, but not yet giving him the position of suitor.

Kandake made herself available for these presentations only two times per week. On those days she did not train, but spent the mornings in council meetings, reviewing reports, or sitting with Aunt Alodia studying Nubia's history and diplomacy.

She had hoped to put off entertaining Prince Gadarat long enough that he would need to return to his kingdom. It did not happen as she planned. He was the first to present himself on the third week of her entertaining.

Prince Gadarat walked through the doorway without acknowledging the warriors and took the seat across from Kandake. Where the others had sat straight and tall within this chair, demonstrating their respect for the occasion, the prince lounged.

"Prince Gadarat, I am pleased to have you visit," Kandake said. *Only because tradition dictates I say that I am. But, we will see how long I am able to tolerate your presence.*

_13_

"Would you care for refreshment?" Kandake asked. She poured pomegranate juice into a bowl made of red clay with a black rim—a Nubian design.

Prince Gadarat accepted the vessel from her, covering her hand with his. Kandake extricated her hand without looking at him and dropped it into her lap. He sipped the beverage with a slight upturn of the corners of his mouth.

"May I end your hunger?" Prince Gadarat placed a few slices of cheese and a honeyed fig onto the dish. He offered it to Kandake but did not release it when she took hold of the plate. "Please, permit me." He picked up the fig and held it out for her to bite.

Kandake let go of the plate, placed both hands in her lap, and leaned back in her chair away from him.

"Prince, it is not our custom that you should touch me, nor should you attempt a thing as intimate as offering me food from your hand. Since I am not your wife," *Thank the gods!*

"It is not the accepted behavior." She leveled her gaze with his. "This meeting is only to allow you to state your desire to become *one* of my suitors and inform me of your ability to provide for a family and of your qualities that would attract me to you. At that time I either accept or *reject* your attention."

He set the plate down. "It was not my desire to offend, Queen Kandake." Amusement hovered around the edges of Prince Gadarat's voice. He sat back, watching her. His gaze shifted to the warriors standing near the wall some distance behind Kandake. He paused, then said, "Oh, yes, this is where I tell you my qualities that should make me attractive."

I doubt there could be any. You are beyond arrogant. Kandake guided herself through a calming exercise in her mind.

"I am the first son of Zoskales, King of Aksum. His rule will be mine, as will his wealth. I have been told that I am very pleasant to look upon. I am not so old that I could not produce many sons, nor am I so young that others do not obey me." He pulled an object from a pocket within his robes and set it upon the table in front of Kandake. "I brought this for you. It is crafted by the greatest artisans of Aksum. It would please me to see you wear it."

Kandake stared at the object, an armband made of gold, fashioned in the likeness of a cobra with eyes of shiny blue lapis; with the snake swallowing its tail.

"When my father told me we were coming to Nubia, I commanded it to be made that I might offer this gift to the most beautiful Princess of Nubia. I had no idea I would have an opportunity to sit with Nubia's queen."

"I am sorry, Prince Gadarat," Kandake said. "Tradition states that I may only receive gifts from my suitors. If you will take it with you, you may offer it to me on an afternoon when you return."

"Of course," Prince Gadarat said, scooping up the piece as he stood. "Our customs and traditions make us who we are."

Kandake would have thought the man had been offended had it not been for the smirk on his face. "When you return, then," Kandake said, standing with him. It took every ounce of discipline she had to refrain from folding her arms across her chest—a gesture that meant he was rejected as a suitor. It took equal effort to clasp her hands behind her back, inviting his return.

I love Nubia. I love her people. I love her culture, but I do not always love her traditions!

14

"Can you believe that arrogant pig wanted me to eat from his hand?" Kandake fumed. She and Ezena walked beyond the stables to share their evening meal so as not to be overheard.

"What? Does he not understand what that means, that you would share his bed?" Ezena asked. "Maybe there was some misunderstanding."

"I cannot be sure. When I told him it was improper, his response led me to believe he understood. Nothing would give me greater pleasure than to erase that smirk from his face…permanently!"

"What do Natasen and Kashta have to say about it? Were they not there to post shield?"

"They were there, but when Gadarat left, I was too angry to speak with anyone." She tore off a piece of bread and passed the loaf to her friend.

"You followed tradition. You allowed him to present himself, now you do not have to see him again." Ezena waved her hand in a dismissive fashion and passed the bladder of water to Kandake.

"Yes, I do." A note of resignation tinged Kandake's voice. "Alara believes it is a good idea for me to keep seeing him so that I can find out what he and his father have in their minds relating to this kingdom." She took a long drink. "It is unfortunate, but I agree with my brother. Prince Gadarat is planning something and I would like to know what it is."

"Do you believe he would tell you?"

"Not in the beginning. He does not respect the strength or the ability of women. For this reason, he will not guard his words with me." She put an olive in her mouth and rolled it over her tongue, enjoying its brininess.

Ezena touched her friend's arm in sympathy. "I do not see your time with him being pleasant." She shook her head. "How many other suitors have you chosen?"

"There will be five in all." She ticked them off on her fingers as she named them. "Amhara, of course, Nedjeh's brother Semna, Irike, and Nesiptah." Kandake pulled her knees up under her chin.

"The only warrior among them is Amhara. Did not others present themselves?"

"They did, but I kept comparing them to Amhara and he outshines them all." She could not hide the smile she felt cross her face.

"Do they know yet?" Ezena asked her friend. She sucked on the chewing stick she had used to clean her teeth.

"No, I must get Great Mother's approval before they can be told." Together, Kandake and Ezena cleared the remnants of their meal and returned to the palace. "Amhara will be advancing to journeyman status soon. Uncle Dakká promised to tell me when he plans the ceremony so that I can be sure to be there."

"He must pass the assessment, first," Ezena said. "If he does not…."

"Of course he will pass. I see him practicing some mornings when I am training with Uncle Dakká."

"Amhara is a strong warrior, but you see the man, not his skill," her friend teased.

At the entrance to the palace, Kandake and Ezena parted ways. Kandake headed in the direction of her grandmother's rooms.

Now that Kandake sat the throne, it was not necessary that she bow at Great Mother's door for permission to enter, but she did so, proffering the respect due the woman.

"Thank you for such honor, My Queen," Great Mother said. "It is a pleasure and privilege that you would visit. Come sit with me." Seated on a large pillow near her window, she gazed at her view of the kingdom.

Kandake gave her a packet of honeyed figs—her grandmother's favorite.

"You have received many suitors. Who have you selected to entertain?" her grandmother asked.

"I have chosen five." Kandake listed the names as she had done with Ezena. She watched her grandmother's face for her reaction to each name. Great Mother's expression revealed little of what she thought except for her quizzical look when Kandake named the prince of Aksum.

"I would not have thought Prince Gadarat to be to your liking."

"You are most correct. He is not! I do not trust him—neither does Father. Alara believes I should accept him as a suitor to gain understanding of his plans and desires about Nubia, and I agree." Kandake balled her fists is frustration and displeasure then forced herself to relax them. "He is not a man that respects women, nor does he believe in my ability or right to rule. It is because of this that he cannot like who I am. That tells me he has other reasons for presenting himself. I would know what those reasons are."

"That is wise, My Queen." Her grandmother retrieved the scroll of papyrus on which she had written the names of potential suitors for Kandake. "I see Semna's name listed here and so is Irike's, but I do not have Nesiptah's. He is older than the others and yet you accepted him?"

"He is older, yes, Great Mother, but he is kind and gentle." She rubbed some of her grandmother's scented oil over her arms. "His company would be a welcome respite following a difficult day."

"There are those who will say that you chose him because of his many cows."

"I have no need of his cows. Our herds are large enough."

Her grandmother nodded and referred back to her list. "Neither Semna nor Irike are warriors. I would have thought you would have chosen others like Amhara."

"There is no one like Amhara," Kandake said. Her feelings for the young warrior filled her. "If I choose a warrior, it will be him."

"Tell me why you have chosen Semna and Irike."

"Semna is an artisan, a very good one." *Ezena would say that he is not as good as her Nateka.* "He is also very generous. I have seen him give his wares to those who have nothing to trade. Irike is a hard worker. He labors long after others have finished for the day. Although he is often very tired, there is still laughter in his heart. This he shares with all around him."

Great Mother set aside her papyrus sheets. "That brings us to the young warrior. Tell me about him."

Kandake did not attempt to keep the smile from her face. "Amhara is a strong warrior. He is eager to learn new skills and works hard to perfect each one. He loves Nubia and is willing to do whatever is required to protect her. His loyalty is without question." She stared off into space envisioning the young man.

"These are all strong attributes, but that alone is not why I have chosen him. I made the decision to accept him as a suitor because of the man that he is. Amhara is honest." Kandake's heart filled to bursting. "His mistakes are his own. He never allows another to be blamed for something he has done. His word can be counted upon. When Amhara tells you he will do a thing, it is done. If his support is needed, he is unshakeable."

"I am sure the fact that he is pleasant to look at is not a part of your decision."

Kandake giggled. "There is that."

15

Kandake walked into the council chambers ready to begin a new day. She had arrived before anyone else. The quiet of the room suited her. Maps of surrounding kingdoms covered the walls. Rolled hides, papyrus scrolls, and clay tablets cluttered the tables and shelves at the far side of the room. These contained records of the transactions of her father's reign. She sorted through them until she found the one she needed—Aksum.

She tugged loose the thin leather thong that tied the rolled hide and spread it over the top of the table. It obscured much of the view of the table's inlaid map of Nubia. She read through her father's dealings with King Zoskales. They all covered the same theme— King Zoskales trying to take something that belonged to Nubia.

"It is no wonder Father calls the man greedy!" *The son is so much like his father. Could two men be more unpleasant?* Members of the council entering the room interrupted her reading.

"Good morning, My Queen," Uncle Naqa said, taking his seat. "What is that you are reading?"

"I am looking into the business conducted between Nubia and Aksum."

"Doing business with King Zoskales is more like protecting the kingdom from thieves. He moved the border between our kingdoms just to lay claim to our herds."

"He would do that?" Kandake looked to her uncle to see if this was a joke.

"He has done it more than one time." Uncle Naqa laid his finger on the place in the record addressing the issue.

As she read, the others entered the room. Deep in concentration, she did not stop to greet them.

"Good morning, My Queen," Aunt Alodia said. "What record has captured your attention?"

"She is gaining an understanding of that scoundrel, Zoskales, from Aksum," Uncle Naqa said.

"What questions do you have, My Queen?" Aunt Alodia asked. "I may be able to clear up any confusion."

"Father referred to the king of Aksum as a greedy man. I was wondering why."

"Because he grabs whatever he can for his kingdom without any thought for who might own it." Uncle Naqa spat. "He would swallow Nubia whole if given the chance."

"I believe that to be his intent. Allowing Gadarat present himself for you to choose as a suitor, My Queen, he hopes for a marriage." Alara said, taking the seat nearest hers. "Have you decided whether or not you will accept him?"

"Why would she not accept him?" Tabiry said. "He is a handsome man and one day he will wear his father's crown."

"His face is pleasant enough, but his body has little strength. He will wear Aksum's crown, but none of that is why I have accepted his company." Kandake rolled the hide and set it aside. "When we first met, he impressed me as an arrogant man. Sitting with him for that short time has changed my opinion. To say that the prince is arrogant would be a compliment. That man believes the sun rises for his pleasure alone and that the moon should be his pillow!"

"And still you will entertain him, My Queen?" Uncle Naqa said. Distaste and disbelief engraved sharp lines on his face. "May I ask why?"

"Because I do not trust him!" She splayed her hands on the table, leaned toward her uncle. "The man has no respect for this kingdom and even less for my crown. I need to know what plans are in his mind, what he hopes to gain. His estimation of women is very low. He is so pompous and overconfident. Because he believes there is no need to guard his words, I will know what he is after."

"That is wise reasoning, My Queen," her aunt said. A smile tugged at the corners of her mouth. "Keep him close. Hear what he has to say."

"That is my plan, though it will not be easy. When he is in my presence, it is a struggle not to plant my foot on his backside and shove with everything in me."

"The prince has requested an audience," Alara said. "He has a proposal to make in the name of his father and wishes to discuss that with you." He tossed a scroll of papyrus onto the table. "It seems Aksum would like to alter our trade agreement."

"In what way?" Uncle Naqa asked. "For as long as I have been Protector of Nubia's wealth, every proposal coming from that kingdom has been to our detriment. The man is a thief, as were his father and his father before him."

"Prince Naqa," Aunt Alodia said, "the queen must come to her own conclusions about Aksum. Your position is to advise her in how the proposal will prosper our kingdom."

"Thank you, Princess Alodia, but I have already come to an understanding about Aksum and its current ruler, through his son," Kandake said, reminding everyone at the table that she was more than an impressionable child. She turned to her brother. "Prince Alara, would you please read Aksum's petition for the council?"

Alara unfurled the sheet and read its contents aloud.

"Is he truly asking Nubia to forfeit trade in frankincense because Aksum does not have trees enough to support their commerce?" Tabiry said, face twisting into an incredulous knot.

"Not exactly, Princess Tabiry. He is proposing that Nubia give them use of our groves for the duration of one harvest season. In exchange, Aksum will give Nubia a number of breeding cows." Alara rolled the scroll closed.

Tabiry's mouth worked like a fish out of water as she tried to get her words out. Uncle Naqa was the one to speak.

"Did I not say the man is a thief?" Uncle Naqa shouted. "He requests the use of the groves for only one season, but the moment he learns their location, his warriors will encamp there and never relinquish them. And you can be sure the cows he sends will be old and sick."

"Only Nubian warriors will ever control any part of this kingdom or its holdings." Uncle Dakká said, his fist thumping the table.

Kandake examined the faces of the council members. *The proposal is absurd. I would never agree to something like this. It is certain Father would not. Why is everyone getting so excited? Do they believe I am so young that I cannot see?*

"There is no need for argument," Kandake said. "It is obvious that this proposal is not in Nubia's best interest. There is only for us to decide the manner of our response."

"Queen Kandake is correct," Aunt Alodia said. "Let us look at the entire situation."

"Thank you, Princess Alodia." Kandake turned to her uncle. "Prince Naqa, does Aksum possess anything that would be of value to Nubia?"

"There is copper. Our artisans could use it for jewelry and dishes or to increase our bronze production."

"Aksum's proposal is not acceptable." Kandake sat back in her seat and folded her hands in front of her. "It is not my desire to start a war between the two kingdoms by denying their request out of hand. So, it must appear that Nubia is taking their appeal into consideration. I propose we counter it by asking the same of their copper mines, and tin as well."

"What do we need of their mines?" Uncle Dakká demanded.

"That is the point," Kandake said. "Our mines provide gold and iron enough. Yet, if Nubia had control of Aksum's mines, it would give our warriors a substantial foothold well within the kingdom of Aksum and effectively end much of their trade and add to ours."

"King Zoskales would never agree to such a proposition," Uncle Naqa said. "How would it benefit his kingdom?"

"It would not," Kandake said.

"But if there were a marriage between Queen Kandake and Prince Gadarat…,"Aunt Alodia said.

"Then he would have control of it all. I told you the man is a thief." Uncle Naqa ground his teeth. The click and slide could be heard across the table.

"With a marriage between our queen and their prince it would not matter whose warriors were in which kingdom!" Uncle Dakká shouted. "Prince Naqa is correct. The man is not to be trusted. He is a thief and a scoundrel!"

Kandake turned to Alara. "What hope could he have had that Father would agree to such an arrangement?"

"I do not believe he did," Alara said. "He is confident that his son will win the queen's admiration and persuade her to marry him. Then he would have the groves and much more."

"And that will happen when the moon replaces the sun!" Kandake exclaimed. *I am liking this prince less and less.* "But it would be interesting to see how far this prince is willing to go to gain my affection. Watching him try could even be entertaining."

"You must not offer him offense," Aunt Alodia said. "That could provoke war."

"He is not careful that he does not offend me. When it was time for him to offer me food, he attempted to have me eat from his hand and he offered me a gift."

"I saw the offense," Natasen said, nodding. "Had Kashta not held me back, I would have bled him like the pig he is!"

"It is important that we take care in considering Nubia's response to Prince Gadarat. While he is a guest in this kingdom, no harm may come to him." Aunt Alodia turned to her brother. "Prince Dakká, is it possible that he could be doing these things to cause conflict between Nubia and Aksum?"

"That is a consideration," Uncle Dakká said. "It is common knowledge Nubia has committed to assist Egypt. With a substantial number of warriors there, King Zoskales could believe Nubia's attentions are divided. Because of that, Aksum could suppose there is the possibility of conquering this kingdom."

"Never!" Kandake and Natasen shouted.

16

The following morning, Kandake held audiences for the people of Nubia who had business with the queen. As the last to request an interview, Prince Gadarat bowed before her. She acknowledged him and directed that he rise.

"Queen Kandake," Prince Gadarat said. "It is my great pleasure that Nubia would take the time for a conference with Aksum. I, Prince Gadarat, the next to rule that kingdom, am gratified by the presence of your beauty. I consider it an honor to be counted among your suitors."

"Prince Gadarat," Kandake said. "This is not the place or the time for such a private topic of conversation. Today we are two kingdoms—neighbors that may have business to discuss. What is it you seek from the throne of Nubia?"

"I ask your pardon. It is not my desire to offend. The beauty of Nubia's throne overwhelms me."

Kurru, standing to the rear of the Aksum prince, moved to offer him a more physical correction. The tight shake of Kandake's head in the negative belayed his action.

You are not sorry. The expression on your face and the lines of your body speak arrogance and prerogative, not regret!

"You would do well to keep our customs in mind," she said. "Again, I ask, what business has Aksum with Nubia this day?"

"Aksum presents a petition to Nubia that would be of benefit to both kingdoms. May I offer you this scroll?"

At Kandake's nod, Kurru accepted the rolled petition from the prince and handed it to her. She set it on the table at her side.

"I am aware of Aksum's request."

"Then may I have Nubia's response?"

"Nubia is not prepared to respond at this time. It requires careful consideration." She saw the smirk that the prince did not quite keep from his face. "Aksum will have Nubia's answer soon."

"When can we expect a reply?" he pressed, taking a step toward the throne.

Kurru came to stand in front of Gadarat, facing him. The warrior took two long strides, forcing the prince to move backwards and away from Kandake.

"Prince of Aksum!" Kandake said, her voice as sharp as the edge of her blade. "You take more latitude than is proper." *Your intentional disrespect for this*

throne is beyond tolerance. Why? What are you after?
"It is clear that the day's heat weighs heavily upon
you. I can think of no other reason for such rudeness.
Please go and take your rest." *Before I leave the queen
behind and introduce you to the warrior.*

Kandake walked into the council chamber. It
required every measure of control she possessed not to
slam, kick, or throw something.

"Please, send a runner for Prince Dakká. You will
find him in the warrior's compound." Kandake said.
As the servant walked through the doorway to obey
the request, Kandake called her back. "No, send a
runner for Prince Alara instead."

"What a fool!" Kandake paced from one end of
the chamber to the other. "Does he want war between
our kingdoms?"

"Does who want war?" Alara said, entering the
room.

"Prince Gadarat! Uncle Naqa calls his father a
thief, but the son is a half-wit. What good would war
serve either kingdom?"

"What has he done now?"

"He requested an audience to formally present
Aksum's petition. Before he did, he began what should
be a private conversation—in the throne room!" She
turned and paced the other direction. "Then he pressed
for Nubia's response to that request." She flung her
arm in the direction of the table at the scroll of
papyrus. "When I informed him it would be some time
before Nubia answered, he advanced on the

throne…the insult!" Kandake stood in front of Alara. "Is the man trying to provoke Nubia or just me?"

"In most cases that would be the same thing," her brother said. "What makes you think this one is different?"

"I am not certain. That is why I called for you instead of Uncle Dakká." She took a seat at the table. "When King Zoskales addresses Father, there is respect for Nubia's strength, even though the man believes he is the more clever one." She poured water for Alara and for herself. "When his son faces me, he does little to disguise his sneer. It was much the same when he presented."

Kandake's brother drank his water, set the cup aside, and said, "I am glad you called for me. Our uncle would not take this well. Then things would not be well for anyone in either kingdom."

"There is considerable difference in his behavior with Father. As my anger cools, it becomes clear that this man is more fool than I first supposed. In his failure to guard his words and thoughts, he forgets that his behavior reflects on his kingdom. It will be a very sad day when his father dies."

"Yes, My Queen. It will be a very sad day."

"But today his father lives and Gadarat is only the prince. I believe I know exactly how Nubia will respond to Aksum's request. We will discuss it at the next council meeting." She reached across the table and took hold of her brother's hand. "Thank you for being who you are. Great Mother chose well for me. Talking things over with you has always helped."

"What will you do about the prince?"

"I have a plan for him. I will entertain him as a suitor, but it will not be as he hopes." She allowed a grin to develop across her face; one she was sure portrayed more predator than pleasure. "He will learn about the strength of a Nubian woman and a warrior."

17

Kandake walked with Amhara to a shaded area within a copse of acacias. When they sat, he offered her a cool drink from the bladder he carried. Kashta and Natasen rested some distance from them, but close enough to respond if needed.

"It is a fine day, My Queen," Amhara said, looking around. "I come here often to think through things when I am puzzled. These trees provide respite from the afternoon sun and the breeze is cooled by the waters of the river."

"It is very comfortable and peaceful here. I can see why you would use this as a place for sorting your thoughts." Kandake rested her back against a tree. She inhaled the scents of Nubia: the aroma of healthy cattle, the metallic tang of smelting iron, and the fragrance of cooking fires. *What could be better than this?* She focused on Amhara's face. *Nothing.*

The conversation they shared was easy and pleasant. She told him about the long hours she had to put in to maintain her training with Uncle Dakká. He talked about his upcoming advancement and the new skills he was learning. Then they spoke of the hunts they had shared and the areas that were best to find the largest game.

"I have brought you something," Amhara said, when there was a lull in their conversation. He held out a small package to Kandake.

"What is this?" She lifted it from his hand. "I was not expecting a gift. Our time together pleases me enough."

"It is something I believe will be of good use should you undertake any more rescue ventures." He smiled as wide as his mouth could stretch, but he had a mischievous twinkle in his eyes.

A new bowstring bound whatever Amhara had concealed within a patch of hide. Kandake unfolded the tanned bit of animal skin to reveal a coil of thin strips of leather woven into a fine braid. A multi-colored glass bead was tied to one end of the braid and a small, bronze disc had been affixed to the other. A wedge had been sliced from the circle of the disc, which extended to the pierced center of the piece. A relief of fat cattle and tall grain decorated the surface of the brown metal.

"It is beautiful." Kandake reached to pluck up the bronze piece from its wrapping.

"Be careful how you handle it, My Queen," Amhara warned. "The edges of the cut-out are very sharp. Lift it by the outside rim or at the center where it is pierced."

"It has the look of an ornament for my hair," she said.

"It is that, but it is also a tool that can be used as a weapon if needed." He took the disc. With the braided tail in his hand, Amhara demonstrated its use, twirling it in tight circles. The disc whistled as it cut through the air.

"This leather braid is meant to tie the hair. The bead acts as a fastener. It slides though the opening at the wedge and hooks in at the center." He looped the thong around several fingers a few times and secured the bead. "This is how it is intended to be worn."

"May I try it now?"

"It would be my honor."

Kandake pulled a layer of her braids to the back of her head in tail fashion. She attempted to tie it as Amhara had instructed, but fumbled each effort. "Natasen," Kandake called to her brother. "Would you help me?" She would have preferred to ask Amhara to assist her, but tradition dictated that such intimacy occur only if she was choosing him to be her husband.

Kandake instructed her brother in the use and handling of the ornament. She held her hair while he tied Amhara's gift in place.

"Thank you, Amhara," Kandake said, as her brother walked back to his seat next to Kashta.

"My Queen," Kashta called from the small distance. "We must return to the palace."

"Thank you," she said. Kandake and Amhara stood, signaling the end of their afternoon together.

"May I walk with you?" Amhara asked.

On their way to the palace, Kandake and Amhara talked about the training that was scheduled to take place within the next few days. *This has been such an enjoyable afternoon. I doubt time with any other suitor will be as pleasant.*

Kandake walked to her rooms to find Ezena waiting for her. Still riding on excitement from her time with Amhara, she was eager to share it with her friend.

"Spending time with your cousin was wonderful!" Kandake passed the dish of sliced meats to Ezena.

"Tell me everything," Ezena pushed her meal aside and leaned toward her friend.

"We walked away from the palace, beyond the stables. We talked about training, the new skills he is learning, and then he gave me this." She pulled the ornament from her hair. "Be careful, the edges are sharp," Kandake said as her friend lifted it from her hand.

Ezena traced the engraved scene with her finger. "It is beautiful." She turned it over looking for the artisans identifying mark on the back. "It is Nateka's work." She tested its edge. "This is as keen as a blade."

"It is more than an ornament, it is also a weapon. Let me show you." She demonstrated its use for her friend.

"Up close, you could cause great injury to an enemy's eyes. It is sharp enough to slice through rope or leather bindings." Ezena fingered the device. "Yet, it is so beautiful."

"I have never seen anything like it." Kandake looped the tether around her braids. She nicked her finger sliding the bead into place. "Now all I have to do is learn how to fasten it properly without carving off a finger." She sucked at the cut to stop its bleeding.

"Who do you entertain next?"

"Nesiptah," Kandake said. "He has requested to share a meal with me. I have a council meeting in two days. It should finish about midday. We will eat together then."

"Is he not ten years your senior?" her friend asked. "Why would you consider someone that old?"

"Nesiptah is kind and gentle. It would be pleasant to have an evening with him after a long day of difficult decisions. Add to that, he is not so old that he cannot father children."

"I thought you were not interested in children." Ezena said with playful scolding.

"I was not interested in receiving suitors or marriage, either. But I will admit, both ideas appeal to me—maybe not right away."

Ezena grinned. "I see."

Kandake enjoyed the light conversation and gentle teasing. Over their meal, they discussed their suitors and what they liked about each one.

"Have you entertained Prince Gadarat, yet?"

"No, I have not." She felt her dislike of the idea pull at her face.

"You will have to do it soon," Ezena said, encouraging her friend. "Just see the man and have it done."

"Why spoil a delicious meal by talking about that…."

A servant burst through the door and bowed at Kandake's side. "My Queen, your pardon please."

"What is it?" Kandake granted her permission to speak.

"It is your father, My Queen. Your mother has requested you come to his rooms. She asks that you come quickly."

"I am sorry, Ezena," Kandake said, rising to leave. "I must go. You stay as long as you like. Please finish."

Kandake ran through the palace corridors to her father's rooms. Everyone she passed along the way lowered themselves in respect for their queen. Kandake did not take the time to respond, but hurried all the more.

She stopped at the doorway of her father's rooms. The sight before her wrenched her heart and mind. All of the members of her family surrounded his bed. He lay with eyes closed, body unmoving. The healer stood near her father's head.

A solemn expression fixed on every face in the room. She looked at Tabiry. Her sister was not wailing, but there was terror carved into her features. The scene in front of Kandake was all that she feared, the day she had prayed would never come.

18

No! Father! No! Kandake's mind screamed over and over.

She entered the room on legs that felt as if they were slogging through a mire of sand and clay. Before she could reach her father's bedside, everyone dropped to one knee. Acknowledgement of her rule had become a part of her life since this illness had developed within her father, but this time the weight of her crown was near to unbearable.

"My Queen," her mother said after Kandake accepted their honor. "Come, stand with me."

She moved to her mother's side. The pain of a thousand arrows pierced her heart. She struggled to speak. "My father?" She tore her eyes from her father's still form and searched her mother's face.

"Your father was sleeping. I tried to rouse him for evening meal, but I could not. I sent for the healer."

Kandake turned toward the healer. Her throat tightened, every breath fought for passage.

"My Queen, your father is very ill. It has caused a deep slumber, one from which he may not awaken."

Her father still lived. The relief overwhelmed her. Then the healer's words broke through her elation.

Father, you must wake up. You cannot die.

Days crawled by. Her father's condition did not improve. All in the kingdom maintained their daily routine, but the strain of his illness wrote itself into every word, motion, and face of its people. Kandake continued with her schedule, as well. It was her misfortune that entertaining Prince Gadarat was part of that agenda.

She chose to meet with him in a shaded portion of the palace courtyard. A short distance away, Kashta and Natasen stood shield.

"Queen Kandake, it is good of you to see me during this time of difficulty," Prince Gadarat said. "Your desire that we should share time does me great honor."

"In this kingdom, when a promise is made, that promise is kept," she said. *Unfortunately.*

"How is your father? Is there any change?"

"There has been none, but the healer is hopeful." She searched the sky as if confirmation of that hope would come from that direction.

"The burden of ruling this kingdom alone must weigh heavily upon you. I would be honored and pleased if you allowed me to assist."

While he spoke, she shifted her gaze to a fat insect trudging over a large rock. *I am sure it would please you, but the chances of that happening are the same as that trundle bug carrying that stone.*

"I am not alone. The council assists with all matters of the throne."

"I am certain that they offer you great support, but the final decisions remain yours. A strong shoulder to lean upon is welcome aid to any woman." He attempted to drape his arm across Kandake's shoulder.

"You will keep with Nubian tradition, Prince Gadarat," Kandake said, leaning forward, avoiding the contact. "You are not my husband, nor are you family."

"I am confident that in this time of need," the prince said, glancing over his shoulder toward Kashta and Natasen. "That Nubian tradition and protocol can be suspended."

"Neither tradition nor protocol will be 'suspended', as you suggest," Kandake said through bared teeth. "They are all that restrain the warrior within me."

"Your words are strong, young queen," Prince Gadarat smirked. "Much too strong for a woman of your beauty. It would be better if you allowed a man to assist you. And, as I am the Prince of Aksum, I am fully qualified to fit into that role. You should allow me to make those difficult decisions for you."

Kandake stared at the man. Indignation swelled. Rage boiled, churned. She used every measure of discipline to keep her hand away from the blade she wore against her skin.

You push me too far, Prince. Soon I will not have the ability to restrain myself. My heart longs to wipe that grin from your face, forever! Kandake forced herself to take slow, even breaths. It was only her strength of will that stilled the rage that threatened to cause her hands to tremble.

"Prince Gadarat," Kandake said, her tone gentled by the force of her will alone. "Why is it you assume every woman is weak? I have spent little time with the women of Aksum, but I can assure you, Nubia has very few women of the type you describe."

"Queen Kandake, I do not label women, as you say. It is a truth known by all that a woman cannot do the things that should be left to the men."

"What things would those be?"

"The more difficult things like ruling a kingdom, using the weapons of war, those types of things."

"So it is your belief that Nubia is at a disadvantage having me sit the throne?"

"I mean you no offense. I am certain that your father has trained you well, but…."

"But you feel the throne would be better left to a man."

"I regret that I must say that is true. Nubia has allowed its women many freedoms that could leave her at risk. How can your warriors perform their duties adequately if their attentions are split between fighting with the enemy and protecting the woman who stands next to him?"

"So you do not believe in the skill of Nubia's warriors?"

The prince gave Kandake one of the sneers she had come to expect from him. Only a well-placed tongue between Kandake's teeth kept her from grinding them to nothing.

"Would you care to put that belief to a test?" she challenged him. "Perhaps a spar between one of Nubia's female warriors against one of Aksum's warriors?"

"It is not my intention to insult the great warriors of Nubia. All I am saying is that Nubia might be better served by having a man on its throne. Or, if you must rule, you should have the advantage of having a man at your side."

"Would you be this man?" *I am certain that you believe that you are the man.*

"Nubia could do much worse."

I doubt that. "I see." An idea blossomed within Kandake's mind. "It occurs to me that there is only one way to settle this. To display my strength in a manner that should remove all of your doubt." *While providing for me the opportunity to do what I have wanted to since the first time my eyes were offended by your presence!*

"There is no way to change the truth, but I am willing to hear this out." He leaned against the back of the bench and gave Kandake his full attention. Amusement danced over his face.

19

"I have a proposal for you," Kandake said. "It would provide you an opportunity to convince me that you may be the man to assist me." She used all of the charm she could muster, imitating the behavior Tabiry used with her suitors.

"What would I need to do?" Prince Gadarat asked, leaning toward Kandake. He reeked of eagerness.

So, now I have your attention. "It is your opinion that women are weak. You also believe that a woman could not be an effective warrior. And since I am a woman, you must believe that I am weaker than you are."

"I would not dare to say that you are weak, Queen Kandake. I meant that you could use the assistance of a man."

"And you should provide that assistance?" Kandake watched the grin spread over the man's face. *For once, your arrogance will serve someone other than yourself.*

"It would be my pleasure."

"What if you and I were to spar together?"

Natasen stood and glared at his sister. She waved him back to his seat.

"Spar with you?" Gadarat's look of surprise mixed with incredulity confirmed his contempt for women. "Why would I spar with you?"

"It is what you said. You believe that a man is stronger than a woman and that a female warrior could not be as effective as a male. Since I am both, a female and a warrior, our sparring together should settle the matter for both of us."

"I am certain it would not be a fair contest. I have some training as a warrior and if I were to injure you, it could cause serious conflict between Nubia and Aksum."

"It would not have to. We both will rule our kingdoms. That makes us equals and if we choose to do this, no one can say either kingdom has attacked the other. To ensure that end, we will sign a compact that states, regardless of the outcome, neither kingdom will be held responsible."

This time Kashta stood. Kandake waved him back to his seat.

"Are you sure this is what you want? Does not your tradition dictate that I not touch you?" Arrogance filled his words.

"All will be well, provided you sign the treaty."

"Should I agree, when would this take place?"

"At a time of your choosing," Kandake said.

Which could not be soon enough!

"I do not like this, My Queen," Uncle Dakká said. "What if you are harmed?" His words matched the faces of those sitting around the council table.

"It is not a conflict in which one of us will be killed," Kandake said. "It is no more than what I do in training with any warrior."

"I still do not like it. Your father would not be pleased."

"No, he would not. But this is something I must do, not only because it will give me pleasure"—a grin tugged at the corners of her mouth—"but it will convince Aksum of Nubia's strength while Father is ill."

"So you admit it, My Queen," Tabiry spat. "You are doing this to satisfy yourself."

"There is that, but the greater good of this is that it will remind Aksum to tread lightly at our borders."

"My Queen," Aunt Alodia said. "If one of you is injured, there could be dire consequences for both kingdoms."

"That is why I have asked you to make allowances for that in the treaty you produce."

"I agree with Prince Dakká," Natasen said. He glared at his sister. "Why not allow another warrior do this? I could do it."

"No you could not, nor could any other warrior. If anyone else sparred with the prince, it could be interpreted as Nubia attacking Aksum."

"What about his request of tying Aksum's proposal to the outcome of this contest?" Alara asked.

"It will not come to that. There is no doubt that I will defeat him. His body is soft."

"Do not be overconfident, My Queen," Uncle Dakká said. "The warriors of Aksum are good fighters."

"My Queen," Uncle Naqa interjected. "I wish to discuss how you have tied the kingdom to the outcome. You propose that we counter the prince's request of Nubia's frankincense groves with our use of their mines. Nubia does not have need of Aksum's copper." The expression on Uncle Naqa's face displayed clear displeasure of this arrangement. "And holding the land that surrounds their mines will require that Nubia commit to building and providing for outposts in that area."

"That is not a commitment Nubia should make at this time." Uncle Dakká warned. "While we have warriors away giving assistance in Egypt and warriors here keeping that war outside our borders, it would not be wise to take on such a venture."

"There is another option," Alara suggested. "If Nubia were to gain the rights to those mines and the lands surrounding them, granting those titles back to Aksum would put them in our debt."

Alara's suggestion quieted the council members. Aunt Alodia stared at her nephew. Her eyes sparkled with pride. Uncle Naqa and Tabiry put their heads together and whispered over the figures he was scratching across a sheet of papyrus. Uncle Dakká and Natasen stared at each other, grinning and nodding.

"What is your opinion of this contest and the queen's abilities?" Aunt Alodia asked, looking at Uncle Dakká. "And what are the real chances of the queen being injured?"

"I have not seen the prince fight, but our queen's skills are much better than her rank suggests." Pride washed over his face as he looked at Kandake.

"Prince Alara and I will begin working on that treaty. We will include Prince Gadarat's proposal as requested, but we will counter it with our own." Aunt Alodia gathered her pages of notes.

"While you are doing that," Uncle Dakká said. "Natasen and I will construct the guidelines, requirements, and limitations of the challenge."

Finally, an opportunity to do something about Prince Gadarat's sneer.

20

Kandake broke away from her routine duties and made her way to the warriors' compound to practice. Inside the main building, she found Amhara and Ezena working on one of the more advanced holds.

"That looks very smooth," Kandake said.

Ezena released her cousin, grabbed Kandake by the hand, and led her to a corner where they could talk without being overheard. "Is it true that you and Prince Gadarat will spar?"

"Yes, it is. That is why I am here—to get prepared."

"But why? Everyone in the kingdom is wondering what would cause you to do such a thing."

"I could no longer tolerate his patronizing view of women." Kandake did not even try to disguise her contempt for the prince of Aksum.

"But to challenge him?" Incredulity rode Ezena's words.

"So it is true, you have challenged the prince of Aksum," Amhara said, joining them. "He only scoffs at Nubian women as warriors because he has never faced one," Amhara said, looking at Kandake. "I understand that this prince needs a lesson in Nubian culture and value, but do you have to be the one to mete it out?"

"I want to be the one," Kandake said. Her muscles twitched in anticipation of doling out the much-needed understanding.

""Do you have any knowledge of the prince's fighting skills?" Ezena asked.

"No, I do not know anything about it, but the look of him says he does little in the way of fighting or hard work." Disapproval underscored each word. "Great strength in his arms or legs is not apparent. He has the bearing of one who has things done for him rather than doing them himself."

"Do not let his look fool you, My Queen," Amhara said. "Aksum's warriors are known for their determination in battle. This one has that air about him. He is used to having things the way he wishes."

"My wish at this moment, My Queen," Uncle Dakká said, joining the three friends, "is for you to begin what you came here to do—practice."

Kandake moved to the center of the sparring floor. Her friends stepped to the side-lines to observe.

"Do not think that you two have finished for the day," Uncle Dakká said to Amhara and Ezena. "You will spar with the queen in turn. Ezena, I want you to face Queen Kandake with all speed and cunning. Amhara, when it is your turn, I would have you use all of your strength and skill against the queen."

"My Prince, would it not be better for someone else to face Queen Kandake?" Amhara asked. "She has accepted me as her suitor and we have begun to share our time together."

Uncle Dakká shook his head. "Who better to test the queen than someone who has been her friend and one that wishes to be chosen by her? I can think of no other sparring partner with a greater investment in her success."

Kandake made adjustments to her breastplate and stretched in preparation for the work ahead. At the Prime Warrior's direction, Ezena entered the combat area with Kandake. The two circled, each looking for an opening to strike. Ezena lunged at Kandake. She aimed her shoulder at her opponent's midsection.

Kandake took the blow allowing her body to fold over Ezena's back. She pushed off with her toes, slid the length of her friend's bent form, and ended her move in a forward roll. She used the momentum of the tumble to drive herself to her feet. She spun to face her opponent.

Ezena closed the distance between them. Kandake took advantage of the shortened distance and punched her. Ezena rocked backwards and countered with her own strikes. Kandake blocked the first blow, but missed the second one. It hit her neck. Pain brought sparks of light to her vision. When Ezena threw the next punch, Kandake anticipated the movement. She caught her friend's arm, pulled Ezena off balance, and swept her feet from under her.

Kandake maintained her hold on Ezena's arm as her friend fell. When she got close to the floor, Kandake released her hold, straddled Ezena, and pinned her shoulders to the surface.

"Release," Uncle Dakká called. "That was very good, My Queen. Now try it with Amhara. He is about the same height and weight as the prince."

Kandake extended a hand to Ezena, helping her to stand.

"Your skill has grown, My Queen," Ezena said. "I remember a time when the blow to your neck would have slowed your response."

Kandake nodded and smiled at her friend's praise. Sweat glistened on her skin. "Uncle Dakká trains me most mornings. One of the seniors takes his place when I have afternoon sessions."

"Your first inclination," Uncle Dakká said to Amhara, "will be to gentle your holds and strikes. This is something you must not do. If you care for the queen, you want her skills to be at their best. Anything less will get her hurt or killed. Do you understand?"

"I understand, My Prince," Amhara said. He walked onto the sparring floor and took a position in front of Kandake.

Instead of circling her as Ezena did, Amhara walked straight at Kandake. He raised a fist to strike.

Kandake struggled to think of him as an opponent rather than her suitor. She prepared to block a punch, but he lowered his stance and swept her feet from under her with his leg. She landed seated on her tail-bone. It surprised her that she misread his intentions.

Get your mind off of his smile and back where it needs to be—on taking him down.

Amhara stepped behind her, where she sat on the floor. He wrapped his arms around her neck and shoulders. Kandake reached for his knees. She grasped them and pulled hard, using the counterbalance to swing her legs up and scissor them around his neck. Now she pushed against his knees, pulled on the back of his head with her heels, and sent him flying over her.

The moment Amhara lay sprawled on the floor, Kandake scrambled to her feet. The movement brought her mind into sharp focus. If she did not use her skills, she would be hurt. This time when he came at her, Kandake moved toward him. She struck with both fists to his belly.

Amhara *umphed* as the strike drove breath out of his mouth. He used the force to turn himself into Kandake's side. He grabbed hold of the back of her neck and threw her to the floor. Kandake rolled onto her back and rammed both feet into his abdomen as he came at her, putting him down—hard.

"Enough," Uncle Dakká said. "My Queen, it appears you have been paying attention to your instruction and practicing what you learn." He reached down and gave Kandake a hand up.

"I would agree with that," Amhara said, rubbing his middle.

"We have time for two more practice sessions before you face Prince Gadarat," Uncle Dakká said. "I would like to increase the intensity of the practice. Tomorrow you will spar with me."

"Yes, Uncle," Kandake said. She released the fastenings of her breastplate and wiped her body with a softened square of hide. Then she swallowed a long drink of water.

Fighting with Amhara was hard enough. She glanced at her uncle. *Now you expect me to spar with you, Prime Warrior of Nubia?* She shook her head. *If I survive this preparation, Prince Gadarat had better concede early on or the lesson I teach will be a difficult one.*

21

Kandake entered Aunt Alodia's room and seated herself at the table in preparation for her studies.

"Today we will examine the ramifications of this challenge between you and Prince Gadarat," her aunt said. She cleared the table of the hides and tablets Kandake's lessons usually came from and sat across the table from her. "He is a man with a large portion of arrogance and pride."

"It will give me great pleasure to carve some of that away," Kandake said.

"That is what we must discuss, My Queen. Prince Gadarat will have difficulty accepting defeat at the hands of a woman, particularly one as young as you."

"You cannot be suggesting that I allow him to defeat me?"

"Not at all. It will be good for him to see true strength—and have that lesson come from a woman. It is important that we project, with reasonable accuracy, the prince's response to being defeated." Aunt Alodia placed a blank sheet of papyrus before Kandake. "I want you to make a list of the possible effects this will have on Prince Gadarat."

Kandake straightened the sheet in front of her, dipped her brush in the inkpot, and gathered her thoughts. *I know what I would like for him to take with him when we spar—a sore back, removal of his smirk, and a trim of that arrogance.*

"The first thing would be for him to gain respect for the strength of women." Kandake spoke as she scrawled across the page. "The next would be recognition that he is not the most important person." She paused, then said, "Better manners." Kandake pushed the paper toward her aunt. "This is what I believe the outcome will be."

Aunt Alodia looked the page over. "Is this what you believe will happen or what you want to happen?"

"I do not see how there could be any other result." She shrugged her shoulders.

"What have you learned about the prince in the time you have spent with him?"

"He is arrogant. He is prideful." She raised a finger for each attribute she ascribed to Gadarat. "He believes women do not have the ability to make good decisions, think for themselves, or have the strength to stand in battle."

"Since you know these things about the prince, tell me how will defeating him in this challenge change how he thinks?"

Kandake looked at the list she had written. "Maybe he will not be so arrogant and he will see that women are not afraid of battle." *Knocking him down may not change him, but it will make me feel a lot better.*

"I doubt that this will change his arrogance," her aunt said. "While it may give him a different view of women as having the ability to be effective warriors, how will this serve to aid Nubia's relationship with Aksum?"

Kandake turned the question over in her mind. "I am not certain that it will."

"Then how is this event necessary for the queen of Nubia?" Aunt Alodia held Kandake's gaze waiting for a response. "My Queen, in everything you do, there must be little doubt of the effect your actions have on this kingdom."

Kandake opened her mouth to speak, but her aunt forestalled her comments with an upheld hand.

"The challenge you have presented Prince Gadarat will benefit Nubia in this way: Should you defeat him, he will have to rethink his opinion of Nubian women as weak. Even should the unthinkable happen and you lose, your confronting him with obvious skill will also cause him to reconsider his views." A sly grin spread across her aunt's face, a gleam, with a touch of wickedness, entered her eyes. "What you will have gained for Nubia is certain knowledge that her queen is strong and underestimating her is a deadly mistake."

Aunt Alodia's praise and certain confidence encouraged Kandake. She sat taller in her seat, her back straight and her head held high.

"Be wary of one thing, My Queen. This man will not take defeat well."

_22_

Early the next morning, Kandake began her day in the warriors' compound. She stood in the center of the sparring floor facing her uncle.

"Now, My Queen," Uncle Dakká said. "I will attack and you defend."

Her uncle came at her straight on.

Kandake had never experienced her uncle as an opponent. She had watched him spar with many of the senior warriors and had admired his skills. The strength of his body and the determined expression he wore during those times had always appeared formidable. She had even had the opportunity to fight alongside him when bandits attacked the caravan they were escorting. But never before had she faced him in this position. Everything she believed about his abilities came crashing in on her.

It is no wonder Uncle Dakká rarely loses a challenge, he has all of the ferocity of an angry rhinoceros. In that moment, all of Kandake's determination, all of her confidence evaporated.

For the first time, Kandake found herself unable to move in the face of an opponent. Her uncle advanced on her, but she could not take action. She knew she should respond, but could not give her body a clear command. Her muscles sang with anticipation, but without direction they were useless.

He was on her, raising his powerful fist to strike. She had to avoid the terrible blow. Kandake dropped to the floor. Her bottom connected with the polished wood slats with a thud. Now she was in danger of the man's strong legs and feet. Not only was she vulnerable to his kick, he could choose to stomp her. Kandake rolled onto her side and coiled her body in a protective knot waiting for what she knew would come.

"Rise, My Queen." Uncle Dakká bent down, extending a hand to assist her. "Do you suppose the Prince will stop his attack because you curl yourself into a ball and lay helpless?"

Kandake stared at the floor. What could she say? *Uncle, you frightened me so I did not move. What is wrong with me?* Kandake raised her gaze to meet his. "I…you…."

"My Queen," Uncle Dakká said, placing a hand on her shoulder. "When an opponent frightens you or appears stronger, that is when you fight the hardest."

She felt tears prick her eyes. *Do not cry!* she ordered herself. *You are not Tabiry.* "I know Uncle. It is just…"

"It is not good enough to know, My Queen. You must put that knowledge into action."

Kandake's chin fell to her chest. "I know," she mumbled. Her embarrassment bordered on shame.

"Tell me, My Queen." Her uncle spoke in encouraging tones. "When we were attacked by bandits and the one larger than myself came at you, how did you respond?"

"I fought back."

"Why?"

"Because he would have killed me. He said as much."

"And when you fought the challenge with Shen? He certainly meant to punish you, if not to take your life." Uncle Dakká lifted Kandake's chin and looked into her eyes.

"I fought because if I did not, my brother and all that were with us may have died. I could not allow that to happen."

"In these two instances, were you not afraid?"

"I was very afraid."

"So what stopped you today?"

Kandake searched her mind. "It was something in your eyes. That something said you could hurt me without really trying and that you would if I did not stop you. And at that instant, you were larger and stronger than I could ever believe."

"Did not the two men you fought have that same look?"

"No, My Prince, they did not. Their eyes told me that they were angry. It said that they had no respect for whatever skill I might have. It is the look I see every time I am with Prince Gadarat. It pushes me to a determination that I will not fail. I will do whatever I can to change that look."

"My Queen, it is good that you are able to use that, but it is nothing more than an anger of your own. Please understand, the men you fought, it was their anger that betrayed them. It caused them to underestimate their opponent and it will do the same to you." Uncle Dakká placed both hands on her shoulders. "I have taught you to fight without anger. Use your knowledge and training to fuel your moves. Read your opponent, assess his abilities and use that to your advantage."

He moved away from her. "I will come at you again. Read my body. Watch how it moves. That will tell you where and how I will strike. It will also tell you how to avoid and how to counter whatever I do."

Uncle Dakká came at her again, this time she met him block for blow. She was able to return a few of her own. She was even able to knock him off of his feet a time or two.

"That is what I am talking about, My Queen. My skill level has not changed, neither has yours. As your ability to read your opponent increases, so will your ability to meet whatever challenge presents itself." He swiped sweat from his eyes with the back of his hand.

"Do not allow your emotions to drive or direct you. They will lie to you about the one you face. Emotions exaggerate and mislead you when determining the abilities of your adversary, making them appear much more or much less than they are." He called a halt to their practice.

Kandake's body dripped with sweat. Her muscles quivered from the exertion. Leaving the compound, she came upon Ezena.

"Do you have time for a swim?" she asked her friend. A dip into the cool waters of the Nile was exactly what her tired body needed.

"I was coming to find you," Ezena said. "It seems that Prince Gadarat is telling anyone who will listen, that once he puts you down, you will have no choice but to marry him or risk war with Aksum."

23

Kandake awoke with mixed feelings about facing Prince Gadarat. Was this a battle she could win? Was he a capable warrior? The soft look of his muscles suggested he was not. The challenge would take place in the early afternoon. She spared little time for her appearance beyond being clean and neat. There was much she needed to accomplish before the match. But of the many things that Kandake had listed, a visit to her father ranked most important.

She walked the halls of the palace taking in all that reminded her of Nubia's strength. Kandake trailed a hand along the wall engraving of a Nubian trade caravan as she passed by. The walls depicted evidence of the kingdom's profitable exchange. She walked near a table upon which set several figurines carved from cedar. She lifted one to her nose and inhaled. The rich, pungent scent of the wood filled her nostrils. It always reminded her of time spent with her father. When Kandake was very young, she would sit at the king's feet while he carved her a new plaything. She took the piece with her instead of returning it to the table.

Kandake arrived at the doorway to his rooms. Her mother knelt on the floor beside the bed with her head resting next to her father's.

"How is he?" Kandake asked. "Has there been any change?" She crossed the room to kneel next to her mother.

"Very little," her mother said, wiping tears from her face. "The healer says your father is resting well and that his body is not as hot as it was."

"Is that good?"

"He says that it is a sign that your father is fighting the illness, but there is still a chance that his spirit will leave him."

Kandake laid her arm across her mother's shoulders to comfort her.

"The healer says that we must talk to him to keep his spirit here." Kandake's mother heaved a huge sigh. "I have been talking to him through most of the night. I fear for him, Kandake. I do not want to lose him."

"We will not lose him, Mother. Father is strong. He will fight." She smoothed stray strands from her mother's face. Dark rings around her eyes told Kandake that her mother had spent more than one night talking to him. "Please, Mother, go rest. I will talk to Father."

"You cannot, there are many things you must see to."

"The kingdom will wait for me while I am here. It will be fine." Kandake attempted to lift her mother from the floor.

"No," Her mother pulled away from her. "I will not leave. He needs me."

"Very well, Mother, you stay." Kandake eased her mother back to the spot where she had been. "But you must rest." Kandake directed servants to bring blankets for her mother and food to eat.

After she had settled her mother, Kandake knelt next to her father and began speaking. "Father, today I meet that Aksumite on the sparring floor. He is larger than I am, and likely to be stronger, too. I am not worried because his arrogance will cause him to underestimate my abilities." She rearranged the blankets around her father and checked to see that her mother was eating. "I am not saying that the victory will be won without difficulty. It is that his overconfidence will lead him to poor decisions that will work in my favor."

She lifted her father's hand and laid the back of it against her cheek. "Prince Gadarat misjudges most things. He expects the world to be as he thinks it should, not what it is."

Kandake looked at the covered window and imagined the view beyond it. "It will not be long before the Nile recedes and the planting will be done. Nuri has staked out her new location in the manner in which she wants to build. Bricks are being baked. By the time that area is cleared of stones and grasses there should be enough bricks to start the foundation."

She talked to her father as if he heard and understood all that she said until it was time for her to leave. "I brought you something," she said, rising from the floor. "It is a cedar giraffe. Remember how you would carve things for me and tell me stories? I will place it next to your head. Think of me when its scent comes to you." She placed a kiss upon his brow, arranged the covers around her sleeping mother, and left the room.

Father, I have never coveted your crown. Now that I wear my own, there are times when its weight feels like more than I can bear. She stopped walking and leaned her back against the wall just outside the entrance. *I had hoped to speak more about the challenge, but I did not want to worry Mother. Father I am worried. I sparred with Uncle Dakká in practice. When he advanced on me, my fear turned my arms and legs to stone. It made a soup of my mind.*

Uncle says that I must not let my emotions dictate my course. I never thought that was me or my way of viewing life. Now I am not certain. Am I more like Tabiry than I think? Did I allow my impatience with Prince Gadarat to create a situation for Nubia that we will all regret? Please, Father, you must awaken. This crown may require more than I am.

<u>24</u>

Kandake entered the main building of the warrior compound. To get inside, she had to walk through a large crowd of the kingdom's people. She wound her way among the growing group as she headed in the direction of one of the small rooms to change clothes. She had assumed there would be some interested in watching the challenge, but she did not expect that there would be this many. Aunt Alodia met her at the door.

"My Queen," she said. "I have the treaty for you and Prince Gadarat to sign." She held it out for Kandake to read. "I have added a provision. It states, regardless of the outcome, that neither kingdom will hold the other answerable for any injury that may occur during this contest—barring death."

Kandake took the scroll and read it through. "This is good. I would not want King Zoskales accusing Nubia of bringing harm to his son."

"Prince Dakká and I thought it best to limit the number of people who may observe. There will be five for each side."

"Why so many? There is only need for two—one from each side to determine the outcome and to verify the victor." Kandake fastened her breastplate into place. She twisted and reached to get a feel for her range of movement and comfort. She adjusted the straps.

"Five is the number of warriors King Zoskales left behind to protect his son. If they are all present, Nubia cannot be faulted for any insult or injury that may result. That also allows for you to have that many protectors, My Queen."

"May I choose them?" When her aunt assented, she said, "I would have Princes Dakká and Natasen, Ezena and Amhara. That leaves one more. Who would you recommend?"

Kandake exchanged her linen skirt for the tanned hide she wore to spar. She wrapped it around her hips and tugged on the tie to ensure the knot would hold.

"I would suggest either Alara or myself to insure that every condition of the treaty is upheld."

"Then I would choose Alara," Kandake said. "I would not want the prince to think that I need my elders for protection or guidance. If members of my own council are present, there can be no misunderstanding of Nubia's confidence in my rule."

"That is wise, My Queen."

Kandake walked into the main room. Her aunt and Alara handed over copies of the treaty for Prince Gadarat to read. After he confirmed that the scrolls were exact replicas, he and Kandake signed both copies—one for each kingdom. Then the five warriors from Aksum spaced themselves along the perimeter of the sparring area. The Nubians stood interspersed among them.

Kandake stretched again before she stepped over the boundary of the sparring floor. When she felt ready, she walked to the center of the area and waited for Prince Gadarat. The prince did very little stretching, but made a show of flexing his muscles and tying the fabric wrapped at his hips tighter.

He swaggered into the sparring area exchanging smirks and grins with one or two of his guards. "A woman should know her place, know where she belongs, and that is not here," he jeered in a voice loud enough to fill the room. "This is a place of strength, a place for men." He walked up to Kandake, but kept his eyes on the Aksumites in attendance. When he reached her, he delivered a back-handed slap across her face. "Now, go where you belong!"

Kandake felt the muscles pull in her neck as her head rocked with the blow. Her eye stung and teared. Rage threatened to consume her. Her first response was to plow into him, knock him to the floor, and stomp him.

This is what Uncle Dakká warned me about. I will not be beaten by my own anger!

She calmed the fury that roiled within her. *I will not allow you to anger me.* Kandake leveled her gaze with his as she brought her emotions under control.

"This is a place of warriors and honor. I am a warrior. This is where I belong." She punctuated her statement with a sweep of his feet and a shove of his shoulders.

Prince Gadarat went down, landing on his backside. He jumped to his feet and ran a toe over the floor where he had stood, as if expecting to find something slick and slippery.

Kandake took a step back, forcing the prince to come to her. This time he appeared attentive and wary in his approach. He crouched and circled to his right. Her positioning mirrored his, sinking low into her stance and matched him step for step.

Gadarat changed his direction, circling to his left. Kandake did the same, stalking him as hunter to prey.

He sprang at her leading with a hammer blow meant for her shoulder. Kandake blocked the strike, pushing it away. She completed the move with a back-handed clout just in front of his ear. Prince Gadarat's head snapped to the side under the force. His left ear nearly touched his shoulder. She spun around firing the flat of her foot into his chest.

They circled each other, trading blow-for-blow. They danced right. They danced left. Each strike dragged at her strength. Each block sucked at her strength. Kandake's arms felt like weighted sacks.

Finally, the prince knocked her to the floor. He moved to straddle her. Kandake met him with a kick to his middle. It knocked him backwards giving her time to regain her feet.

Kandake advanced on Gadarat and gave him three tight, sharp jabs to the face. His nose bled. Though she was tiring, she willed herself to continue. *I will not quit, not until he surrenders.* That one desire pushed her on.

He wiped his face with the back of his hand, and returned her punches with powerful thumps to her midsection forcing her breath to explode from her and bending her forward.

Kandake used the momentum, tucked into a knot at his feet, and rolled forward to bowl him over.

The prince went down hard, smacking the back of his head onto the floor. The thud was loud enough to bounce off of the walls. He lay there, stunned.

Kandake struggled to get to her knees. Sweat flowed from every pore. It streamed into her eyes, stinging and blurring her vision. She crawled over to the prince, his head lolled to one side. She climbed on top of him.

Kandake dug her knees into the fleshy part of the prince's upper arms and pressed her forearm to his neck and leaned on it. She gave the prince a strong dose of pain. She leaned on her forearm making it difficult for him to breathe.

"Yield," she gasped, panting from the exertion. Pain echoed throughout her body.

"Not to a woman. Never!" The prince sneered.

Kandake bore down adding more weight to the arm she had on his neck. "Yield."

"I will not be bested by a woman." The pressure on his neck caused his voice to rasp.

"I am more than a woman. I am a warrior, Queen of Nubia. Yield!" Kandake leaned into his neck harder. She positioned herself, forcing her knees to bite into the muscles of his arms. Kandake delivered as much pain and cut off as much of his breath as she dared. The pressure she applied was just short of producing severe injury to the prince.

Prince Gadarat struggled. He tried to roll Kandake off of him, but she stayed put. He brought up his knees, knocking them into her back, trying to break the hold she had on him. She did not budge.

The downed prince twisted and bent, but nothing he did would dislodge Kandake. She kept him pinned to the floor. At last, when nothing he tried would get her off of him, the prince nodded his head, agreeing to yield. Kandake glanced at her uncle making sure he saw the prince's signal to yield.

Kandake collapsed onto her back, slick with sweat. Her chest heaved for breath. Finally, there would be rest for her tired body, her strained muscles.

Prince Gadarat sat up. "No woman bests me— Prince of Aksum." He threw himself backwards driving the sharp point of his elbow into the base of Kandake's neck and the tip of her collarbone.

Kandake screamed.

<u>25</u>

Kandake lay on the floor. Pain made keeping her eyes open difficult. Every muscle in her body tensed from the strain. Natasen and Amhara ran toward her. Uncle Dakká's barked order stopped them and brought the young warriors back to their place of observation.

Prince Gadarat remained in repose next to Kandake. She watched in pain as an expression of self-satisfaction settled onto his face.

"You have no honor." Kandake panted. Her voice rasped from her injury. "You dishonor your father and your kingdom."

The prince stood, turned his back on Kandake. "I am Prince Gadarat. I will rule Aksum and you will learn your place."

Driving rage put Kandake on her feet. An angry scream ripped from her throat. She jumped onto the prince's back. She wrapped her legs around his waist. Blinding pain raced through her body, but she forced her arms to work. She folded her uninjured right arm around Gadarat's neck. She reached across to his left shoulder and locked her wrist in her grasp. She gave no thought to her own pain. Kandake used her left arm as leverage to cinch the right arm tighter and tighter.

Prince Gadarat fell to his knees. Kandake maintained her constricting hold until the prince lay on his face, unconscious. She released him. Exhausted, she snaked her arm from beneath his limp form. She pushed his slackened body until she rolled him off of her leg. He flopped onto his back.

As she lay beside him she examined his face. *I did it, the sneer is gone!* She allowed herself a brief grin.

In agony, she climbed from the floor to her feet. Shaking, she staggered to her uncle. She collapsed into his arms.

At last the pig is quiet, he has nothing to say.

Uncle Dakká eased Kandake to the floor, checking her from head to toe. Natasen held onto her, supporting her as she assured everyone that her injuries would heal.

The warriors of Aksum walked in a stiff-legged gait to stand before Uncle Dakká. The unit lowered themselves in respect for the Prince. Uncle Dakká glowered down at them, his body rigid with unconcealed rage.

"It is not our place to offer apology," the ranking warrior said. "His behavior has brought shame to us all. We ask your mercy."

"Mercy?" Uncle Dakká's features twisted in fury. The tone of his voice brought to mind the sound of sharpened iron slicing through flesh.

With Natasen's help, Kandake struggled to her feet. She turned to face her uncle. "Prince Dakká, these men cannot be held responsible for the actions of the son of their ruler any more than Prince Natasen can be blamed for mine. It is clear that this is a matter to be worked out between the King of Aksum and the Queen of Nubia." She leaned on her brother. "Please allow these men to take the prince wherever they will that his injuries might be attended."

In her rooms, Kandake sat on a low bench while the healer tied the last strip of the bandage securing herbs to her collarbone.

"It does not appear to be broken, My Queen," the healer said. "No sparring or heavy work with that arm until the swelling goes down."

"Thank you for your service," Kandake said as he packed his supplies to leave.

"Is it true that you almost killed the Prince of Aksum?" Tabiry said, walking through the doorway. "Are you trying to start a war?"

"Thank you for your concern," Kandake said, her words laced with all of the sarcasm she could muster. "The healer says that I will be better after a while."

"What are you talking about?" Tabiry barked. "I heard him say there was nothing broken."

"Please, tell me, dear sister," Kandake said, irritated. "How is it that regardless of what takes place, I am always the one at fault?"

"That is simple to answer. It is because you are always the one doing something wrong. You are the one who challenged Prince Gadarat. You are the one who nearly ended the life of a prince of an allied kingdom."

"I did not come close to ending Prince Gadarat's life nor is Aksum our ally." Kandake looked around her room for something to do—anything that she could use as a reason to end this conversation with her sister.

"Now, you are calling Aksum our enemy. Next you will say that Nubia should go to war with that kingdom." Tabiry glared with her arms folded across her chest.

"Aksum is not our enemy, neither is that kingdom our friend. I am not planning to go to war. Is there anything else I can do for you?"

"You can tell Amhara to stop talking to Shen about what happened between you and the prince."

"What are you talking about? What has Amhara to do with Shen and why should you care?"

"I care because of this," she pointed at Kandake's bandage. "Shen is talking about leaving Nubia. He says that he does not want Nubia to be blamed when he confronts Prince Gadarat about what he calls the prince's dishonorable actions against you."

"I thought you wanted him to leave. Now you want him to stay?"

"Will you not just do as I ask?" She threw her arms into the air as if in exasperated surrender, then settled her hands upon her hips and glowered at Kandake.

Kandake stared back at her sister. Tabiry squirmed beneath Kandake's scrutiny and would not make eye contact. Understanding wound its way through Kandake's mind. The truth of what bothered her sister came as a shock. She could not deny herself the grin that split her face. "You have accepted Shen as a suitor!"

26

"I cannot believe it. Shen presented himself and you accepted him as a suitor!" Kandake felt laughter bubbling up, but she squashed it down.

"Why should I not? He is not that uncomely."

Kandake stared opened-mouthed at Tabiry. "After all of the fuss you made about Shen staying in Nubia, Shen being the wrong everything, and Shen presenting himself, you have accepted him as a suitor."

"Uncle Dakká says that Shen is a good man and that it is an honor to accept his company." Tabiry held her head at a haughty angle. "But that cannot happen if he leaves the kingdom, can it?"

"Tabiry, the man is free to come and go as he likes."

"I have asked you many things, but this is really important to me." Tabiry lowered herself into a position of respect. "Please, My Queen, help me in this. Of all of my suitors, Shen is the man I would choose."

Struck by her sister's sincere plea, Kandake's heart softened toward her. She stood and laid her hand on the back of her sister's head, an indication of Tabiry's favor with the queen. "I will see what I can do." Ignoring the pain, she lifted Tabiry to her feet. Once she got her sister settled, Kandake went in search of Shen.

She found him in the warrior's compound sparring with Kurru, a senior warrior. She waited on the sideline until they had finished. Both men lowered themselves in respect. She gestured for them to stand.

"Shen, when you are free, I would like to speak with you."

"Yes, Queen Kandake. I am available now."

"Shall we walk, then?" Before they left the building, she encouraged him to take a drink of the cool water in the vessel at the back of the room.

Kandake waited until they had left the compound before she began their conversation. "I am told that Amhara shared with you what happened when I sparred with Prince Gadarat."

Shen grunted acknowledgement.

"I also understand that you are planning to confront him."

A sharp nod of his head indicated Kandake was correct in his intentions.

"May we discuss it?"

"There is nothing to discuss, Queen Kandake. The man attacked you."

"That is not quite the truth, Shen. We were sparring."

"But he had conceded the match to you. His actions were not a part of the contest. He intended to harm you."

Kandake watched Shen as he spoke. She remembered the time when he had attempted much the same thing when she stood against him fighting as proxy for his commander. His wince suggested that he likely recalled the same incident. She laid a hand on his arm and stepped in front of him. "You must not do this thing."

"His behavior was outside the bounds of the treaty. He must be punished."

"You would have our two kingdoms go to war over this?"

"I will leave Nubia. Then none can say that this kingdom is involved." His face hardened with his determination.

"But you and I know that Nubia is the reason for your actions. If I pretend otherwise, then I am no better than the prince."

"Queen Kandake, when I escorted you from our encampment back to Nubia, I made a vow then to protect you. I have not renounced it."

"But if your actions bring war to Nubia, is that not a violation of your promise?"

Shen held Kandake's gaze. Evidence of his struggle of conscience tracked across his face.

"As part of that vow, I ask you not to do this."

Shen stared at Kandake for a while longer. His chin dropped to his chest. "I will do as you ask. I will not go against what I have sworn to do."

"Thank you, Shen. You have saved me from Tabiry's wrath." She smiled at him.

"Her wrath?"

The puzzled look on his face made Kandake laugh. "Yes, her wrath. When she found out what you intended to do and that you were planning to leave Nubia, she blamed me."

"She is part of the reason I would do it—to earn her respect."

"My sister is not like us. She is not a warrior. The fact that you have been named as one of her suitors is an indication of her admiration for you."

"She told you that?" he asked in a voice thick with hope.

"Sisters do not tell each other's secrets."

<u>27</u>

Kandake devoted her morning to visiting with her father, meeting with the council, and studying with Aunt Alodia. She had spent the previous afternoon with Semna. Today she would share her midday meal with Amhara.

He met her in a small field not far from a group of children playing a game of stone pitches. Kandake cheered for each child as they pitched flat stones at gourds attempting to knock them over.

"Is that not Kurru's son?" Amhara asked. "His aim is good. He hits the shell just where it meets the ground. That guarantees it will topple every time."

"When I used to play this game, it took me a while to learn about hitting that spot," Kandake said. She pointed to a young girl whose turn it was to pitch.

"My cousin, Nasalsa, seems to have mastered hitting that spot as well."

"She should, I see her practicing with the bow every day."

"Nasalsa desires to be a warrior like her father, Prince Dakká." Kandake turned away from the children to face Amhara. "What is this I hear about you encouraging Shen to retaliate against Prince Gadarat?"

"We did not encourage him," Amhara said, his hand resting over his heart as a sign of his sincerity.

"Who is 'we' and where did Shen get the idea?"

"Natasen and I were practicing with our slings against targets. Shen asked us to help with his aim. His problem is more with his release of the stone. He—"

"Do not change the subject," Kandake said, her tone of voice gentled the words.

Amhara's face took on the expression of a small boy trying to talk his way out of being punished after getting caught sneaking a bite of someone else's sweet treat. "We were talking about the challenge when Shen joined us. We spoke of what the prince did after he had accepted his loss. Shen asked what we had planned to do about it. We told him we could not because it would bring war to the kingdom. We did not tell Shen to do anything."

Kandake searched Amhara's face. "Did you know what he intended to do?"

"He did not tell us of his plans, but we felt certain he would respond in some way."

"And you did not attempt to dissuade him?"

"No I did not. My Queen, it is very difficult for me to allow that man to walk free in this kingdom after harming you. The ones I care for have my protection. I care for you. You are more than my queen."

Kandake sat braiding the grasses next to her as she thought about Amhara's words. *When it is time, I will tell you all that I feel. I am not yet ready to take a husband, but when the time comes…*

"Do you have time for a walk?" Amhara asked. He stood and assisted Kandake to her feet.

"I am free for a while longer, but I would rather play a game of pitches. I am sure I can tip over more gourds than you." She dashed to where the children had been playing, laughing all the way.

Kandake returned to the palace. Alara met her at the entrance.

"My Queen," he said, dipping a knee. "Prince Gadarat has requested an audience to discuss the transfer of the mines."

"Must I do it today? It has been so pleasant, I would like for it to remain so."

"It would be best to do it at this time. He is preparing to leave the kingdom."

"Is he truly leaving? That would make the day even more pleasing. Make him first of this afternoon's audiences. I will see him as soon as I change. I have been playing stone pitches with Amhara," Kandake said.

"Stone pitches, My Queen?"

She laughed and left him to change.

Kandake met with Prince Gadarat. Alara had made good on his promise. The prince of Aksum was the first of her afternoon interviews. "How may I help you?" she asked the prince. *Please tell me quickly so that you may leave this kingdom!*

"You may help me most by behaving like a woman," he said, standing up from dipping his knee. "But I am not sure you have the knowledge."

Neither your arrogance nor your insults will remove the joy I feel at your departure from this kingdom.

"You requested an audience," she said, ignoring his words. "What is it you wish to discuss with the Queen of Nubia?"

"I would prefer to speak with the king. Because he is a man, I would know what to expect. Who knows what thoughts whirl in the head of a woman?"

Two of the warriors within the room advanced upon the prince. Kandake waved them away. "Since you have requested this audience, I think it best we attend to the matter that brought you here."

"Yes, Queen Kandake, that would be best. Before I leave Nubia, I would like to settle the matter of Aksum's mines. For them to be transferred into the care of this kingdom, I must discuss this with King Zoskales. He will determine the time and manner it is to take place."

"That is acceptable," she said. "Nubia will wait for your king's decision."

"I will not be gone long. There is still the subject of your marriage."

"The subject of my marriage?" She stared at the man attempting to understand what he was talking about.

"I will continue as your suitor and as I am certain that I remain the only appropriate choice, I will return to discuss the details of when we are to be wed. In Aksum, you will remember how to be a woman."

_28_

Kandake paced the length of her father's room. "Father, I need you to wake up. The warrior is overtaking the queen." She flailed her arms as she spoke. "The meat in Aksum must be filled with worms, for surely the crawlers have made their way to the prince's head to imagine I would ever marry him."

Kandake moved to her father's side and bathed his brow with cool water. His skin looked dry and cracked. She called for a servant to bring a pot of moisturizing oils. She scooped some of the thick salve into her palm and warmed it between her hands. Its fragrance reminded her of the beauty of Nubia. Kandake applied them to his skin. The aroma filled the room.

"Father, if you do not wake soon, I am afraid I will do something that will not be in the best interest for this kingdom." She smoothed the ointment over the skin of his arm, massaging its length from shoulder to finger-tip. The strength of the muscles within his arm gave her a feeling of pride in him. "Uncle Dakká tells me that you continue to practice your skills. I feel the proof." How she wished her father could hear the praise she offered.

She moved to the other side of his bed. Kandake lifted his other arm and massaged it as she moisturized. "I am not prepared to take a husband now, and if I were, it certainly would not be him." She shook her head.

Kandake took another dollop of the balm into her hand, and again warmed it before applying it to her father's chest. "I am clear on the point of not marrying the man, but I am not sure how to refuse him without causing a problem between the kingdoms." She sat on the small bench next to his bed and laid her head upon his shoulder. "Father, you must awake. Mother needs you. Nubia needs you." Tears slipped from her eyes. "I need you."

"My Queen," Alara said as he entered the room. "How is our father?"

Kandake raised her head, wiping away tears with the back of her hand. "He still sleeps, but his skin feels much cooler." She threw her arms around her brother's neck when he sat next to her and let her tears flow. "Why must everything be so difficult? Father is ill. He has not awakened. There is war at our northern border that threatens to break into Nubia. Aksum requests what it knows we would never give. Their only reason for such behavior is their belief that helping Egypt has weakened us." She mopped at the tears coursing down her face with the edge of her skirt. She took a long, shuddering breath.

"Because I sit the throne, the doubts of Nubia's strength are a question—for Aksum, at least."

"The strength and skill of our warriors has not changed because you are now queen," Alara encouraged. "Neither is Aksum so foolish to believe we would have ever given the frankincense groves to them."

"There is still the question of how and when to give them back the copper mines. And, to make things much worse, that horse's hind-end of a prince believes I will marry him!"

"Are you certain you gave him no encouragement?"

"It has nothing to do with anything that I have said or done. He has declared himself the only viable choice among my suitors, and as such, believes I must marry him. That is one thing that will NEVER happen." Kandake slammed both of her fists onto her thighs.

"If you are that certain, I do not see how his beliefs can be a problem."

"Aunt Alodia says that I must not offend him while letting him know that he is mistaken, which is something he will never accept. The man thinks he is correct in all things!"

Overwhelmed, frustrated and confused, she sobbed into her brother's shoulder. "I fear I will cause more harm to the kingdom than good."

"Little Sister," he murmured, stroking her back. "Things will come right, you will see. Father is strong, he will fight this illness. You have done well in his absence and I cannot see how that would not continue. Nubia is in good hands. Great Mother knew what she was doing naming you as our queen." With gentle hands, he pushed her away from him. He caught her gaze with his own. "Tell me, what are your thoughts for this kingdom?"

"First, Nubia must remain strong. That is the most important thing, no matter who sits the throne. Our borders must be strengthened to the south—a clear message to Aksum that regardless of how we assist Egypt, our warriors protect our lands."

Alara nodded, encouraging her to continue. As she spoke, her tears ceased to flow.

"Next, we must do all we can to restore Father's health. The Master Healer must have everything he desires to aid Father." She reached for the light covering at her father's feet and pulled it back. "Father's skin requires more care than our mother can provide. She divides her time between sitting with him and attending to her own duties." Kandake put more of the salve into her hands. "Caring for our father cannot be Mother's burden, alone. Our father has four children. From now on, one of us will attend to this, daily. We will care for him, not the servants. We will ensure that he is bathed and rubbed with oils. All Mother should have to do is to talk with him, give his spirit a reason to remain."

As Kandake organized her mind around what needed doing, the sorrow, confusion, and doubt that plagued her fell away like chaff slips from wheat during threshing.

"I need your help to turn him so that I may reach the skin of his back." They shifted his body so that he lay on his side. Alara held him there while Kandake slathered a generous portion of the balm onto their father and massaged it in. Together, they lowered him onto the bed and each taking a leg, rubbed the soothing oils into his skin.

"I would like to know how our warriors are faring in Egypt," Kandake said, wiping her hands on a bit of toweling. "Send a runner to inquire after their needs as well as bring information about them for their families."

"It will be done, My Queen," Alara said, smiling at his sister. "Will there be anything else?"

"Yes, call a meeting of the council. I want the matter of Aksum's mines settled before the prince returns."

Alara left the room to see to her requests. Kandake bent to her father's ear.

"I may not do things as you would have, Father, but I promise Nubia will be strong and waiting for you to return to the throne. I will see to it. Now, you see to your health. Get well Father." She laid a gentle hand along the side of his face.

Kandake walked into the council chamber. At the table, she confirmed the presence of all members, took her seat, and began. "I have asked Prince Alara to send a messenger to Egypt." The heads of all seated at the table nodded their affirmation.

"Prince Dakká, I would like you to look into the state of the border we share with Aksum."

"Are we expecting difficulties with that kingdom?" He had a look of mild concern on his face.

"No, we are not," Kandake said. "But I would like Aksum to have an understanding that Nubia is up to strength, regardless of having some of our warriors in Egypt."

Tabiry glowered across the table at Kandake.

Why must she always behave as if I am the cause of all of the difficult things in this life? I do not have the patience for this right now.

"Princess Tabiry, is there something that you would like to say?"

"There is nothing, My Queen." She continued to glower.

"Princess, your face is speaking what is in your heart," Kandake said. "Please, tell us what is causing you such distress."

Tabiry looked at the faces of those seated with her waiting to hear what she had to say. "The question in my heart, My Queen, is this: Are you planning to take this kingdom into war with Aksum because Prince Gadarat struck you?"

29

Princess Tabiry," Kandake said. "I understand your concerns, but at this time Nubia has no plans to go to war with our neighbor or any other kingdom."

"If you increase the number of warriors patrolling our border, will not King Zoskales believe that to be our plan?"

"May I respond to that, My Queen?" Natasen asked. He sat forward to press his point with his querulous sister. "Princess Tabiry, protecting our kingdom's interest is not the same as beginning a war. These actions are taken in hopes to prevent one."

"Why should I believe you?" Tabiry glared at him. "You are just as battle-hungry as she is!"

"Princess Tabiry," Aunt Alodia said. She pitched her voice to a calm and soothing level. "Your queen has told you what is necessary to protect this kingdom.

There are times when war is a must to insure that all of Nubia's citizens continue our way of life." She reached across the table and took hold of Tabiry's hand. "Although that time may be near, it is not yet upon us."

"Does she have even you fooled?" Tears rolled down her cheeks. "How can I be expected to take a husband and have children if Nubia is at war?"

"I promise you, Princess Tabiry," Alara said. "Our queen is not taking us into a war. She is only trying to keep what belongs to this kingdom on our side of the border. If you read the records, you will see that Father has done the same."

"She is not Father!" Tabiry spat. "What of the copper mines in Aksum? If we attempt to take possession of those, surely there will be war." She looked at Kandake with narrowed eyes. "Why did you ever have to make that a part of your challenge with the prince of Aksum? You knew you would defeat him. Prince Gadarat is not a warrior, what harm could he have done you?"

"Princess Tabiry," Kandake growled. "As your younger sister, I tolerated your questions and criticisms. As your Queen—I will not!" Kandake leveled her voice and narrowed her gaze toward Tabiry only. "Take hold of yourself. Do not allow your fears to create what is not!" She signaled for a servant to fill Tabiry's vessel with water. "Now drink—drink all of it. Remember you are a Nubian woman, there is strength within you. Find it! Use it!"

Tabiry put the bowl to her lips and took a tentative sip. Beneath the glare of all at the table, she turned it up and drained it. She settled back in her chair, straightened her back, and lifted her chin.

"As you point out, Princess, there was little chance that Prince Gadarat could defeat me—I am warrior trained." Kandake said. "It was not necessary for me to tie the transfer of Aksum's mines to the challenge." She called for water for herself and drank it down. "I did this because the rulers of that kingdom are fishing for something. I believe it is their hope to snag Nubia within their nets." She spoke to Tabiry, but she moved her gaze around the table, making eye contact with each person in turn.

"My purpose was to put Aksum on the defensive, allow them to feel the power of this kingdom without going to war. Nubia has no need or desire to hold those mines, but the possibility of it gives Aksum pause. They will have to back away from their catch or bring their plans out into the open. We will hold onto the rights to that land until Aksum has shown their true face."

"Thank you, My Queen. I am beginning to understand, but my concerns are still not put to rest." Tabiry schooled her features to the characteristic neutral expression she uses when things do not please her.

Kandake and Ezena lay in the grass near the stables talking. It had been a long, difficult day. Kandake allowed the company of her friend and their easy conversation to soothe and relax her.

"Is that really true?" Kandake asked. "Nuri is entertaining suitors? I had thought she had decided against taking a husband. She has not been a child for some time."

"It is true. I saw her with Irike's father. They ate their evening meal beneath a copse of acacias." Ezena rolled onto her back.

"That will be good for him," Kandake nodded. "His wife has been dead for some years, it is time he had someone to share life with."

"Amhara tells me that Prince Gadarat has decided he is the man you will choose." She turned her head to look into Kandake's eyes. "I wish you could tell my cousin that it is not so. Prince Dakká has reprimanded him several times for twisting the heads off of practice figures."

Before Kandake could respond to her friend, Shen interrupted their conversation.

"Queen Kandake, may I speak with you a moment?" The man's face looked strained. Shen went down on one knee and bowed very low.

"Ezena, your pardon, please, I will return as soon as I can." Kandake got to her feet. "How may I help you?" she asked Shen after they were some distance from Ezena.

"There are two things. I will begin with my friend, as he is very upset. I asked Natasen about the boasts of the prince of Aksum. He says it will not happen. Still my friend worries. I told him to talk to you about it, but he says it is not your custom and he must wait until you have said what you will."

"You are talking about Amhara?"

Shen nodded.

"He is correct, it is not proper for him to ask such a question."

"But Queen Kandake, the man has misery." Shen's face took on the expression of a man who is near to rage. "This prince from Aksum has brought trouble to my only friends in this part of the world. If it were not for my promise to you, I would do something. His neck is crying out for my hands to squeeze it."

"Then it is a good thing that you have given me your word that you would not." She grinned at the picture in her mind of Prince Gadarat's head bursting while Shen's hands pressed in on the stem between the prince's head and shoulders. "You said there was something else."

Shen blew out a breath as his shoulders sagged. "It is your sister, Tabiry. She worries about the coming war between Nubia and Aksum. I have assured her there is no need to worry. Nubia has strong warriors and I will add my strength to this kingdom." He plowed his fist into the palm of his other hand. "Nubia will never be defeated."

He looked around as if trying to find the words to say more. "Queen Kandake, you must say something to her. Tabiry is not a warrior as we are. She does not understand. All day she cries or rages. Both are too much to bear."

Shen truly cares for my sister. She stared at him for some time. *Is this the husband she says she cannot take if there is war?*

"My sister allows her fears to tell her what is. Nubia is not planning to go to war with anyone."

"That is a disappointment."

"You are that eager for battle?" Kandake asked, puzzled by his comment.

"I have no desire for war, but it would have given me an opportunity to deal with Prince Gadarat without breaking my promise. Now I must find another way."

<u>30</u>

Kandake watched Amhara sweep the ground before she laid out the mat they would sit upon. The day was fine—a feather of white clouds had been painted across the blue sky, softening the mid-afternoon heat.

"Tomorrow I will hunt with Natasen and Shen," Amhara said. "We are scouting the northern trail."

"Why not the trail to the south? The game there is larger and promises more meat for the pot."

"It is better to hunt away from Aksum. Natasen is worried that nearing that border will make it too difficult for Shen to hunt only meat." Amhara looked away as he spoke of Aksum, his body tensed.

It would appear Shen is not the only warrior that would have trouble hunting nothing more than meat along that border.

"How is practice going for your advancement to journeyman?" Kandake asked, hoping to move Amhara's mind away from the prince of Aksum. "I have seen some of your work. You look ready."

"Almost, My Queen, there are a few passes I would like to perfect before I ask for the assessment." Tension leached from his body. "Prince Dakká believes I am ready, but I know that I hesitate on those moves. I want to know that I will succeed and earn the advancement."

Kandake nodded. *This is yet another reason I would choose you to share my life—you work hard at all you do.*

A messenger approached Kashta and Natasen, who stood a short distance from Kandake, posting shield. Whatever he said to her brother had Natasen moving in her direction at a run.

"My Queen," Natasen said, barely touching his knee to the ground. "Our father has awakened!"

Without excusing herself, Kandake was on her feet and pumping her legs as fast as she could toward the palace with Natasen speeding next to her.

She and her brother arrived at the doorway to their father's rooms and slowed to a more decorous pace as they entered. Family surrounded the bed. Their father sat propped up by pillows of bright colors. Their mother sat next to him with her arms wrapped around his shoulders. A smile stretched her lips and for the first time in a long while Kandake saw lines of worry fall from her mother's face. The healer stood next to her. The scene before her filled Kandake with such relief she clung to Natasen as they walked to the bed.

As she approached, her aunt Alodia moved to make room for her to stand near his head.

"Father, you are awake," Kandake said. She surveyed every inch of his body. His skin sagged where it had been taut over a well-muscled frame. His face held an expression of extreme fatigue. His eyelids drooped, covering his eyes to near closing. The slow turn of his head toward her voice appeared to cause him pain. A grimace spread across his features.

"My Queen," he said. His voice, no louder than a whisper, croaked like the frogs of the night. His hand trembled as he reached for Kandake. Seeing this weakness in the man she had only ever seen as strong, tore at Kandake's heart. "How is the kingdom?"

"Amani," her mother said. "The healer has said for you not to strain yourself. Please do not try to speak."

Kandake clasped his hand in both of hers. "It is well, Father."

A servant brought a bowl of a thick brown liquid and placed it into the hands of Kandake's mother. She filled a spoon with it and brought it to his lips. He wrinkled his nose and turned his head away.

"You must eat, my husband. The healer says you need this to regain your strength."

"I am not hungry," he said and closed his eyes.

"She is correct," the healer said, indicating Kandake's mother. "It is important you eat to strengthen your body. This illness has weakened you."

Kandake's mother stroked the side of her husband's face. "Eat."

"I must know what happens in our kingdom. How are our warriors faring in Egypt?"

"That can wait. Your stew is getting cold."

He kept his face turned toward Kandake. His eyes appealed for her answer.

"I can talk while you eat, Father," Kandake said. A cushion was brought and settled next to his bed. Kandake positioned herself so he could see her face.

Kandake's mother dished a spoonful of the stew's juice into her father's mouth. Some of it dribbled down his chin.

"Tell me what that thief of Aksum wanted. Why did King Zoskales come to Nubia?" His voice still sounded like the rattle of dried reeds rubbing together. He lifted a trembling hand to wipe his face.

"He asked for something that he will never get," Kandake said. "He wanted the use of our frankincense groves for the length one year and asked that we not trade anything made from the resin for that same period of time."

"What! Worms must be crawling into his head and tunneling through his thoughts if he thinks we would agree to such an arrangement!" Rage contorted his face. His body shook with it.

"Amani, please calm down. Our daughter has dealt with it," Kandake's mother said. She pressed his shoulders back toward the pillows that held him upright when he attempted to lean forward. "You left Nubia in her capable hands."

"Mother is right. I have taken care of the matter."

"How? What did you do?" her father asked, clutching Kandake's hand.

That is enough for today," the healer said. "Your father needs to rest; otherwise the illness will claim him again."

"The healer is right, Father. I will come back tomorrow after you have rested." Kandake leaned forward, kissed her father's brow, and left the room. Tabiry was waiting for her outside the door.

"Do you plan to tell him about the war you are starting with Aksum?" Tabiry said. She folded her arms across her chest. "I wonder what he will think about how you are running this kingdom."

Kandake cupped her hand beneath her sister's elbow and led her some distance from the doorway so that their father would not overhear them. "Princess Tabiry, this is not a conversation to be had outside of the Council." She kept her voice low but it did nothing to reduce its intensity. "You will remember your responsibility to this kingdom."

Tabiry jerked her arm away from Kandake. "I am still the older sister."

"Yes you are, so you should know the weight your words carry."

"I will say what I like, little sister."

"As the younger sister, I had to endure whatever criticism you had to offer. It was my place to listen to you. As your queen, you will hold your tongue as I have commanded."

31

The following morning Kandake walked to her father's rooms to visit a short while before starting her day. She entered as the healer was speaking with her mother.

"It is as I told you. The illness still has a strong hold on him. He must not strain himself."

"I know what you told me, but yesterday he was awake. He ate and visited with all of us." The expression on her mother's face and the lines of her body told Kandake that she was near panic.

"What is the problem?" Kandake asked, announcing her presence. Her mother and the healer made to lower themselves, but she waved them back up. "What is happening with my father?"

"You father sleeps again," her mother said, near panic in her voice. "I came to share the morning's meal with him and I cannot wake him."

Kandake's head snapped in the direction of her father. She stared at him.

No! How can this happen? He had awakened! She looked first at her mother then shifted her gaze to the healer.

"My Queen," the healer said. "Your father continues to be very weak. If he does not rest, the illness will take his spirit from us."

Kandake walked to stand near her father's bed and rested a trembling hand on his brow. The hope she had gained with his waking was slipping away from her with dread trying to take its place. "His skin burns again. What can be done?"

"There is nothing left for us to do. He alone must fight this illness. He requires food and rest." The healer lifted her father's hand and pinched the tips of his fingers. The moan that came from her father was barely heard. "He responds to this pain. This is not the sleep as before." The healer pinched the finger tips again, and once more her father moaned "He must rest. When next he awakens, there must be no excitement."

Kandake entered the council chamber. Everyone rose as she entered. Distracted by worry over her father's condition, she sat without acknowledging them, reached for the nearest tablet and began reading.

As she selected a second tablet she saw that they continued to stand. "I am sorry, please sit." She scanned the faces of the council members, each of them a member of her family. "Have we any news of our warriors in Egypt?"

"There is word from Pharaoh that the war goes well," Aunt Alodia said.

"How can a war go well?" Tabiry mumbled. "People are killed in war. How can there be anything good about that?" She directed her question at her sister.

"What that means, Princess Tabiry," Aunt Alodia said, as Kandake opened her mouth to respond, "is that Egypt is not being overrun by her enemies."

"I know that, but if war comes to this kingdom we know who to blame." Her eyes bore into her sister's.

"We will blame the enemy!" Uncle Dakká glared at Tabiry. She withered beneath his gaze.

"Well, yes, but" Tabiry stammered. "We could be doing more to keep that from happening. What if Aksum…" She looked at Kandake.

"Do you have reason to believe a threat is coming from that direction?" Aunt Alodia asked.

"No, but—"

"Good, then let us return to the matters before us now." Aunt Alodia shuffled the sheets of papyrus she had her notes on. "We must address what the prince of Aksum has said, declaring that you will become his wife upon his return."

"He has said this." Kandake took a long drink of water hoping to rinse away the distaste the subject brought to her mouth. "He is under the impression that he is the only suitable mate for me and that I have no other option but to choose him." The revulsion at such an idea brought chills to her, raising fine bumps along her arms. "Please be assured that I will do no such thing."

"Where would he get the idea?" The lines in Uncle Naqa's forehead creased to near folds. "Are you certain you have not done anything to make him believe this to be so?"

"No! I have not!" Like an arrow, Kandake's mood shot from annoyed to enraged. "If I were choosing at this time, which I am not, he would not even be the last person I would choose."

Natasen and Alara struggled to hide the smirks that were blooming on their faces.

"It appears we may have a problem bubbling within the pot. If this young prince believes you have committed to marriage with him, there could be problems between the two kingdoms."

"Do you see it now? She will bring war here. Something must be done!" Tabiry leaned back in her seat as if she had furnished proof to her argument.

"Something will be done," Aunt Alodia said. "No young man, prince or otherwise, may announce his betrothal to any Nubian woman without that woman's consent."

"I am afraid I must agree with Princess Tabiry," Uncle Naqa said, shaking his head. "Unless Prince Gadarat can be made to see that he is mistaken, a broken promise such as this will surely mean war, unless a substantial gift is offered and accepted."

Caught by Uncle Naqa's statement about a gift to Aksum, Kandake's mind whirred. Something at the back of her mind was clawing its way forward. *A substantial gift, one that is certain to be accepted.* The idea found a small opening and blasted itself into comprehension.

"That is it! They planned this all along. Of all the low—. Uncle Naqa, you called the king of Aksum a scoundrel. That was a compliment. If what I am thinking is true, he is much worse than that."

She leaned toward her uncle seated at the opposite end of the table. "The prince is not mistaken. He is well aware of our customs and it is clear that I have not chosen him. His father readjusted the borders between our kingdoms for a few cattle. Prince Gadarat is setting a trap so that Aksum can claim Nubia for its own.

"This is the lowest trick of all. If I refuse to marry him, his father can claim insult and demand the frankincense groves as repayment. If I were to go ahead with the marriage, he could claim all of Nubia as his own."

"That treacherous, conniving —." Uncle Dakká was on his feet. "This will never happen. I would rather the kingdom go to war than succumb to such deceitful—. The man is worse than a snake with two heads. No matter which end of the serpent you grasp, there is a venomous bite waiting for you!"

"I had called the man a scoundrel," Uncle Naqa pounded the table. "This is worse. The man is a conniving thief!"

All around the table faces expressed outrage and disbelief. All of the faces except Tabiry's—her lips trembled, her eyes welled with tears. She set up a lament that rivaled the scream and wail of the seasons' worst monsoons.

Kandake stared at her sister. She expected Tabiry to be displeased with the direction of the discussion, but this response was beyond her imagination. Especially, since none at the table had suggested actually going to war with Aksum.

"Princess Tabiry!" Kandake bellowed, exasperated with her sister's behavior. "Take hold of yourself. Nothing has been decided, why are you crying?"

"If Nubia goes to war, my marriage ceremony will be ruined!"

32

"Your marriage ceremony? When did you choose?" Kandake stared at her sister. It was the last thing she expected to hear.

"I have not chosen—yet. But I want to." She wiped her face with the tail of her skirt. Her tears smudged the kohl outlining her eyes. "If Nubia goes to war, everyone will be thinking about that and not celebrating with us. Even he will be thinking about it."

"Whoever he is, I am sure you will be all that is on his mind." Questions circled Kandake's mind. She peered into her sister's eyes for hints about the man she had chosen. *Which of your drones will become a part of our family? I hope you choose one that has some ability to think his own thoughts. What kind of children would come from a marriage like that?*

"Not if he is a warrior like you!"

A warrior? Kandake gawked at her sister. Words escaped her. Her mouth hung open. She snapped it shut. *Shen? He is your choice? His mind is definitely his own.*

"Princess Tabiry," Aunt Alodia said. "No one here is planning to go to war with anyone. Who you choose, and when, is up to you."

"I know, but if she—"

Before Tabiry could finish her sentence, Kandake interrupted, "My sister, if a marriage ceremony is what you want, then nothing in this kingdom will prevent it."

"I am not ready to marry." Tabiry straightened in her seat. "Not yet, but I am ready to choose."

Kandake divided her afternoons between holding audiences with the citizens of Nubia, entertaining her suitors, and visits with her father. His condition improved, but he remained weak and required quite a bit of rest.

She often planned her visits to coincide with the time her mother needed to spend attending to her own duties. Today, Kandake sat with her father in the small courtyard that adjoined his rooms. The weather was pleasant and warm. Gentle breezes caressed and cooled them.

"It feels good to have the sun bathe my skin again," her father said. His voice no longer sounding like the rustle of dried reeds, but it had yet to return to its deep, rich tones and the strength it was known for.

He lounged upon a wide couch and watched what he could see of the kingdom.

The people bustled with their daily activities. Whoever passed near enough to get a glimpse of the two waved to him and dipped a knee to Kandake. Voices of children playing reached their ears. The herds moved about lowing and gnawing on the lush grasses.

Kandake sat on a comfortable chair across from him. "It feels good to join you out here, enjoying the air," she said. "Seeing you lying in your bed was nearly too much to endure."

"Your mother says much the same. She fusses about everything. Am I resting enough? Have I eaten enough? Every moment she is around, she is pushing meat or cheese into my mouth."

Kandake laughed, passing him the package of fruit from her mother. "She made me promise to make sure you ate it."

Her father stared at the parcel as if it might contain some onerous thing.

"She means well."

Her father chuckled, accepted the portion of fruit.

"How is the kingdom?" he asked. "What is happening with the people?" He shifted onto his side. Kandake saw the strain this small movement had on her father.

"The kingdom is doing well," Kandake said. "Nuri has moved her work area to the knoll as she wished. She has taken on three apprentices. The hides that they produce are not the quality of hers, but she says that they are learning well. And the most interesting news is that Nuri is entertaining a suitor."

"Three new tanners will be good for Nubia. I wonder why she has not trained— Did you say that Nuri is entertaining suitors?" He lifted himself onto an elbow. "I did not think she was interested in marriage." He removed the fruit pit from his mouth.

"Neither did I, but it appears she is now."

"Are there many?"

"No," Kandake said. "She is only entertaining one man." She watched her father's face shift through a series of expressions. It took work to keep the amusement of his reaction from her face.

"How long must I wait before you tell me his name?" Her father set the fruit aside.

She waited a half beat more. "It is Takida, Irike's father."

"Irike is one of your suitors, is he not?"

"He is," Kandake said. "I can clearly see why Nuri would choose Takida. The father and son are hard workers."

"Do you ever plan to tell me about the prince of Aksum, or must I continue to pretend that I am asleep so that the servants keep talking?" He fixed his gaze upon hers.

It amused Kandake that her father would participate in such a charade. She struggled with what to tell him and what to leave out. She worried that if he became too excited it would affect his health. As he waited for her to speak, his face held the same patient look he had when waiting for her to answer one of his difficult questions.

She had to tell him something. The set of his brow told her he could, and would, wait until she answered no matter how she delayed or circled around the subject.

"Father, everything is being taken care of regarding Prince Gadarat. Everything will soon be settled."

"Yes, but how? Surely, you do not plan to marry him?"

"So you have heard of his boast. And that is all there is to it."

"The servants worry that he will force this marriage upon you and that you will do this to keep the kingdom from war."

"I have no plans to marry the prince. Nor do I plan to go to war over this. So there is no need for you to worry—or the servants."

"You still have not told me what you plan to do about it. Daughter, I will not have you tie yourself to Aksum just to prevent a war. There is another solution! Find it!" Her father began to tremble.

"You are becoming upset. We must not speak of this anymore."

"Yes, I am upset. As soon as my back is turned that Zoskales, and his whelp, attempt to entrap this kingdom through my daughter. I will not have it!"

"Amani, why are you shouting?" Kandake's mother said, coming into the small courtyard. "You must calm yourself." She leveled a look at Kandake that would have scorched her had she not been used to the scrutiny of Uncle Dakká.

"I will, once your daughter has explained to me this ridiculous business of her marrying Prince Gadarat."

"I am marrying no one, Father, and him least of all."

_33_

"Ezena, how exciting! Are you sure?" Kandake alternated between hugging her friend and bouncing up and down beside her. Each time she plopped on the ground, clouds of dust *poofed* from beneath her. "Who else knows?"

They dangled their feet over the edge as they sat on the bank of the Nile River. Ezena and Kandake tossed small pebbles into the water as they talked.

"I have told no one, not even Nateka. You are the first to share my news."

"What do your parents think of him?"

"My mother is smitten with him. She watches him play with my younger brothers and sisters. She is of the mind that he will give her many grandchildren to fawn over. My father is impressed with Nateka's ability to work any metal and the strength of the tools he makes."

"When will you tell your parents?"

"After evening meal. By then the little ones will be asleep and we can talk without disturbance." She turned to face her friend. "How is your father?"

"He gains strength every day. It will not be long before he is able to return to the throne." Kandake climbed to her feet. She dusted the grit and gravel from her skirt. "That is a day that cannot come soon enough."

"What about Prince Gadarat, have you decided what you will do about his return?"

"I have an idea, but it has not come together as a plan, yet." They walked toward the palace. "Maybe at tomorrow's council meeting I will be able to put the resolution into place."

"Amani, you cannot do this," Kandake's mother said. "You are not ready to work. You must wait until you are stronger."

"I will not gain strength lying in this bed—waiting for others to feed me my meals or having my wife bathe and dress me. I must do something."

Kandake listened to the banter between her mother and father. She had come to share the morning meal with her parents before her day began. Their discussion went on, each one expressing their reasons for what her father should do. Not having been asked, she offered no opinion, but she had one. *Father is gaining strength. He is not as weak as before. It will*

not be long before he can return to the throne.
Attending the meeting would be good for him.

"Sake, I am not saying that I am ready to return to ruling the kingdom. I am only suggesting that I begin attending council meetings to become informed of the state of things in Nubia."

"Our daughter has been managing matters well up to this point. I am certain that she can continue for a short while longer."

"I do not doubt her ability to continue, nor am I saying that I am up to the demands of the throne, at least not just yet. I only want to know what is happening."

"I know you, Amani. If you start going to council meetings you will be on that throne within a matter of days." She turned to Kandake. "Say something to your father. Tell him he must wait."

Kandake opened her mouth to speak, but her father cut her off before she could utter a sound.

"I need you to understand that I must do this. It is not only to gather information, but to reassure the people of Nubia that I am getting stronger and support the decisions of our daughter." He walked from where he stood arguing with his wife, and moved to the nearest seat, his forehead covered in a light sheen of perspiration. The weight he had lost during his illness had begun to return, but it was apparent he had not fully regained his strength.

"I still do not like it, my husband, but I understand. Promise me that the moment you tire, you will return to your rooms to rest."

"You have my word, wife of my heart."

Together, Kandake and her father walked the halls of the palace to the council chamber. Everyone they passed dipped a respectful knee, bowed, and greeted them, paying special attention to her father.

With every person we meet, Father stands a little straighter. He's starting to look like his old self.

They entered the chamber. New light came into the eyes of those seated around the table—even Tabiry's characteristic scowl smoothed into a bright smile. He moved a chair to a short measure behind his daughter, insuring that there would be no mistaking his support of Kandake's rule, and sat down.

"How are you feeling, my brother?" Uncle Dakká asked. "It is very good to see you."

"My strength is returning," he said. "I could no longer lie in that bed. My heart longs to hear news of the kingdom."

The council meeting proceeded as usual. News of the war in Egypt relayed that their neighbor to the north would remain strong. Uncle Dakká gave his report of the promotions pending among the warriors. Uncle Naqa submitted an accounting of the state of the kingdom's wealth, and Aunt Alodia spoke to the current situation having to do with Nubia's neighbor to the south, Aksum.

"My Queen, here is the latest draft of the decree returning Aksum's mines and the lands surrounding them."

Kandake read through the text, commenting on the points that had required clarification, making certain everything was as it should be. "You have worded this so that it sounds like the mines have always been a possession of Nubia and that we are proffering a great gift upon that kingdom."

"If you recall, My Queen, the wording of the treaty is such that those properties became connected to the original holdings of this kingdom. So, essentially, we have always owned them."

I would not want to be Prince Gadarat when he explains to his father Nubia's ownership of those lands within Aksum. I would have sympathy for him if he were not such an arrogant, conniving snake.

"All that remains," Aunt Alodia said, "is for us to determine the best timing for the transfer of ownership."

_34_

A little more than a week later, Kandake shared morning meal with her father. It pleased her to see the ease with which he moved about. "Father, you are getting stronger. It is time I returned the kingdom to you," Kandake said. "Now that your strength has returned, there is nothing preventing you."

"That is true, My Queen. It is just that your leadership and the way the people respect you fills me with such pride. I cannot find it within myself to bring that to an end."

"Thank you for your words of praise, but I believe there is more to it than that. Could it be that your afternoons are free and you enjoy spending that time with my mother? Or could it be the fuss she makes over you?"

"There is that, too." He walked to the edge of his courtyard. "You are correct, My Queen. I will miss these days of lessened responsibility. Will tomorrow afternoon be soon enough?"

"Tomorrow afternoon it is." Her voice sounded calm to her ears, but she knew better. Inside, she shouted and cheered. "There is a council meeting in the morning, followed by audiences with our people. That leaves the afternoon free for the ceremony. I will speak with Aunt Alodia and Alara to make the arrangements." *Hurry, tomorrow!*

"Was it difficult telling your other suitors that you had chosen Nateka?" Kandake asked Ezena. They passed food back and forth as they shared evening meal within Kandake's rooms.

"Two of them looked hurt and one of them seemed to be relieved," Ezena said.

"Relieved? Why?"

"I believe it is because when he presented himself, he was of the mind that I would choose not to remain a warrior. He wants a wife that will partner with him in hunting animals for their hides. My bow and tracking would have been an advantage for him." She chuckled.

"Now that you have announced your choice, have you and Nateka decided when your marriage ceremony is to be?"

"That depends on when my grandmother can come. It is important to me to have her there."

"She lives in Aksum with one of your aunts, does she not? Is there some reason they fear the journey?"

"She does not fear it, but my aunt has just given birth and would not be able to travel with her."

"Will you send for her or journey to bring her here yourself?"

"I had thought about going, but with you on the throne, who would go with me?"

"Since my father is regaining his strength, I will not be on the throne for much longer. I could go with you."

"Would you?" Even if you were not still sitting the throne, I would not have asked you to go with me because of the prince and everything."

"That should be settled soon as well."

35

"I cannot believe it. A few more hours and Father would be on the throne and Prince Gadarat would have had his audience with him." Kandake complained to Alara.

"It is unfortunate, My Queen, but as you still rule the kingdom, holding audiences is a part of that. You must deal with him one last time."

"Then I will focus on this being the 'last time' I am obligated to be in the same room with him." She smoothed back her braids, placed her crown on her head, and proceeded to the throne room.

"I will see him first," she told her brother. "It is as Mother says, 'whether it is a food you dislike or a task you find objectionable, take care of it first so that the displeasure does not linger.'"

Alara removed the smirk from his face as he sent a servant to bring the prince in.

"Queen Kandake," Prince Gadarat said, rising to his feet from a respectful bow. "I have returned with my father's response to your claims to Aksum's mines." He passed the sheaf of papers to Alara, who looked it over and handed them to his sister.

Kandake read it through. She stared at the prince. She held onto her anger with a fierce grip. She lowered her voice to just above a whisper and spoke each word in measured cadence. "Your father refers to our marriage as the force binding Nubia to Aksum and that he gladly gives the mines as a gift for our joining. By what authority have you announced this marriage?" She spat the last word.

"When I was last here, I confirmed our plans to be wed." Prince Gadarat said. "All that remains is for us to set the date."

"You forget your place, Prince of Aksum," Kandake snapped, her patience at an end. "In Nubia, these things are at the prerogative of the woman. As I am the woman, it is up to me. I have in no way implied that you are my choice. I have no plans or desire to enter into any marriage agreement. You will tell your father, King Zoskales of Aksum, that you were mistaken. There will be no joining between the two of us." She took a deep breath to still her rising rage.

"Please tell him, that Nubia accepts his release of the mines and the land surrounding them as agreed upon."

Throughout Kandake's discourse, Prince Gadarat's body became more and more rigid. His mouth worked like a fish just caught from the Nile. When she stopped talking, he found his voice. "Queen Kandake, you understood my intentions from the start. I participated as one of your suitors because of Nubia's custom, but there was never any doubt that you would become my wife.

"This rejection and abdication of that arrangement is an insult to the kingdom of Aksum. I demand recompense and it will be of *our* choosing. You have three days to reconsider your response, at which time I will come before you for your answer. After which I will leave this backwards kingdom with either my wife or whatever I have chosen as compensation. As you consider your answer, I would look to the frankincense groves of Nubia." He turned to exit the throne room.

"Prince Gadarat, one moment, please." She turned to her brother. "Prince Alara, would you offer the prince of Aksum the copies of the records I had prepared should the need arise."

Alara passed to Gadarat the stack of papyrus sheets Kandake indicated.

"As you read through them, you will find the agreement you and your father entered into so that Nubia would extend to you the opportunity to present yourself as one of my suitors. It states clearly that there is no commitment to marriage or any other alliance agreed upon between you and me or the kingdoms. It also states that the choice is mine, alone." Kandake leaned back upon her throne, taking full measure of the pleasure it gave her to put an end to this discussion.

Prince Gadarat read through the record pertaining to the nature of their courtship. Kandake watched his face as he reached the part that stated what privileges he did and did not have. He lifted his eyes from his reading and turned a stony-faced glare toward Kandake.

"Please continue your reading. Go to the accord dealing with the spar between us and what properties were offered in forfeit to the winner. There can be no disputing the outcome of that engagement."

He focused his attention upon the other sheaf of papyrus he held. He read it from beginning to end. The rage that roiled from him as he turned his face toward Kandake thickened the air in the room. He stood, ironbound and staring.

"Now that you have full understanding of our positions, let it not be said that Aksum is so 'backwards' as not to pay its debts." Kandake's body vibrated with pleasure, her mind hummed with amusement.

"Queen Kandake, Aksum has never failed to pay its 'debts', nor has it ever failed to acquire what it desires."

36

Kandake stood in the throne room facing her father. The light of health shining in his eyes filled her heart to overflowing. Every member of her family stood on the dais. As many Nubian citizens as could fit packed the room.

It felt as if this day would never arrive. Kandake studied the faces of her family. Each member wore an expression of pure delight. Gone were the shadows from her mother's eyes. She looked from her mother's face to her father's. *I have never given thought to the love between them. I took it for granted that it was strong. My father's illness has taught me that a marriage requires more than love to give it strength. When I marry, I can only pray that mine will be as strong.*

Upon her head rested her crown of braided gold. Fine linen dyed the many hues of autumn with threads of gold draped her form. It flowed from her waist to just above the circle of golden bells worn on her ankle. Shades of rust, brown, deep greens, and dusty yellow-orange wove their way over the fabric's surface. Bracelets of gold and silver danced about her wrists. Of all that she wore, nothing was as beautiful as the burnished ebony of her skin, rubbed and polished to perfection.

Her father's garment complemented hers. The fabric that hung about his hips was fine linen splashed with the beauty of Nubia's grand sunset. The colors of flame, orange, gold, and purple swirled and swayed over the cloth alluding to the transition that was taking place.

Kandake grasped her father's right hand and gazed upon his proud face. "Father, I return to you what you have entrusted to me. It has been my pleasure to serve you as I have served the great kingdom of Nubia. Please, accept from me what is yours."

She removed from her hand the ring of gold with the large stone of lapis that represented the kingdom and slipped it on the middle finger of her father's right hand. Once she had done this, Kandake lifted her own crown from her head and wrapped it in a waiting square of linen. She tied the parcel with a single wire of gold signaling an end to her rule. She lowered herself to one knee, and bowed before her father. "It has been my honor to serve you, My King."

King Amani laid his hand upon the back of Kandake's head, conferring honor upon her. "Princess Kandake, you have made me proud. Nubia has received great benefit from your hand. I have no doubt that when it is your turn to rule, this kingdom will experience more of the same."

Kandake stood. Great Mother placed her son's crown upon him. She nestled it over the tight, deep, shining curls of his hair. As one, all within the room dropped to one knee, bowing their heads toward the ground.

When released to rise, cheers, whistles, laughter, and calls of delight rang throughout the space.

Kandake embraced her father. "This has been a day filled with joy," she whispered. "And I am truly glad that it is not my turn to rule."

As with all Nubian celebrations, the feasting began. Kandake took her seat to the right of her father. The intensity of her hunger surprised her. She layered her plate with meats and cheeses. She added a few radishes and onions and topped the pile with a hard roll of bread.

She looked at the plate in front of her father. Its tower of food rivaled hers in portions of meat, cheese and fresh vegetables. A plate laden with slabs of bread slathered with butter and honey set next to that. Kandake looked from his plate to her mother, then to her father's face.

"She continues to feed me," her father said. He shrugged his shoulders and a boyish grin plastered itself over his face.

"I understand that our guest from Aksum has left the kingdom," her father whispered. "It has been reported that he was not very happy at the time of his departure."

"He is gone." It was Kandake's turn to shrug and grin.

Later that evening, Kandake walked along the banks of the great river. Alara accompanied her.

"It is a pleasant evening," she said. "Everything is as it should be."

"Yes, it is. Even that bothersome prince has left Nubia."

"You are always more kind than anyone deserves. Prince Gadarat was more than bothersome," Kandake said. "The man is dangerous and so is his father. The point is, neither of them is in the kingdom now, so they cannot cause any more trouble."

"Little sister, you are a warrior. You know a man does not need to be close to you to bring you harm."

"But they are not warriors and we are not at war."

"Do not underestimate your enemy."

37

"Have you and Nateka decided the time of your marriage ceremony?" Kandake asked, taking a short break from target practice. It felt good to be away from the duties of the throne.

"We are planning it for four moons from today," Ezena said, nocking an arrow to her bow. "That will give us time to go to Aksum, get my grandmother packed and come back early enough to prepare everything." She let her shot fly. Its flight was straight and true.

"Us? Nateka is going with you?" Kandake rubbed her perspiration-slick fingers in the dust of the ground. It dried them and increased the surface tension between her fingers and the bowstring, insuring a more secure grip. She let go of the arrow and it flew to the center of the target.

"No, you are. You told me if I waited until you were no longer sitting the throne, you would go with me." Ezena picked up another arrow. "Your time on the throne has not decreased your accuracy."

"That is because I never stopped practicing. When that pompous horse's hind-end was the most insufferable, I visualized his face at the center of the target. It worked every time." She and her friend laughed. Kandake sobered. "I did promise, and since I am no longer wearing the crown, when do we leave?"

"I have to wait until my mother gathers the gifts for my grandmother and my aunt. That should take her a few days. I will leave right after that."

Having each completed two sheaves of arrows, both loosened their bowstrings and walked to retrieve what they had shot from the targets.

"Good," Kandake said. "That gives me time to talk Father into allowing me to travel." She pulled her last shot from the bale of straw. "I will ask him this afternoon when I complete my lesson with him."

"Have you heard that Amhara's assessment is this afternoon?"

"I know. I will be sure to word my request with great care. Otherwise, Father will lecture me long enough to miss the entire assessment period." At the edge of the warrior compound, they separated, Kandake walked toward the palace to prepare for her session with her father and Ezena toward her home to begin preparations for their journey.

"But Father, I gave Ezena my word that I would travel with her," Kandake pleaded.

"It is not safe for you to travel alone at this time. I cannot allow it." King Amani rolled the remainder of the hides that comprised Kandake's lesson.

"I will not be alone, I will be with Ezena."

"As you say, two young women traveling alone during a time when one of our neighbors is at war and the other neighbor may wish to start one." He tied the last of the hides and placed it on the shelf at the back of the council chamber. "Add to that, I am not certain of how King Zoskales plans to respond to the loss of his property. Knowing that jackal, he will not take the loss without some reaction."

"What if I were carrying the accord that returns the mines and the lands around them to Aksum? That would make my safety an important factor to him." Kandake walked with him back to the table. *Please Father, you have to let me go. I have been tied to the palace ever since you became ill. I need to get out.*

"That is a possibility, but I still do not want you to take that journey alone." King Amani sat down hard in the nearest chair. He mopped his brow.

"Father," Kandake dropped to her knees next to him. She reached up and laid her hand along his cheek. "Has the illness returned?"

"No, it has not," he said, a mirthless smile met his lips. "It has not completely left me." He took hold of his daughter's hand. "That is another reason I am reluctant to allow you to go to Aksum. I am tempted to keep you close in case I need you to help me again."

"Then I will stay."

"It is also the reason you must go."

"What do you mean?" She sat in the chair across from him. The icy fingers of fear and panic reached for her.

"If I keep you limited to Nubia, King Zoskales is likely to assume I continue to be weak. He will use that to fuel his greed for all that is within this kingdom. So I have decided to permit you to go with your friend."

"Thank you, Father. Are you sure you do not need me?" Her father's permitting the journey with Ezena should have had Kandake bouncing with joy, but her concern for his health weighed her down.

"I am permitting it with the condition that our warriors accompany you."

"Will not a contingent of warriors provoke the same questions you are attempting to avoid? Or worse, King Zoskales could misinterpret the reason for the warriors."

"There is that possibility, but I will not let you go without protection. That is the only way I will allow it."

"If my safety is your main concern, there is a way to do it without rousing the suspicion of King Zoskales." Her father drew breath to speak, Kandake continued. "But, Father, before you object, let me tell you what I have in mind."

He waited.

"You said you would give your consent provided I had protection. Ezena is a warrior and if Natasen, Amhara, and Shen came along, I would have four warriors to protect me."

"Natasen will be Prime and Shen has proven himself," King Amani said, nodding. "But Amhara is one of your suitors. It is not appropriate for you to be alone with him."

"I will not be ALONE with him—Ezena, Natasen, and Shen will be there."

"That is not the same. You must have someone to post shield or an elder accompany you."

"But...."

"That is my final word."

His face had closed. Kandake knew there would be no use arguing with him. Her father had spoken and her only option was to find a way to get it done—a way that worked for her as well.

"Father has given permission for me to go, provided I take someone along to post shield or an elder." Kandake whispered to Ezena as they watched Amhara on the sparring floor. "If I ask Uncle Dakká, he is likely to choose warriors who will turn the journey into one long lesson."

"So ask an elder," Ezena said. She kept her eyes on her cousin.

"I thought of that, but who should I ask?" Kandake grimaced when Amhara took an extra step on one of his moves. His form had been flawless up to that point. He added a block and hold to utilize the change in positioning the step gave him. From there he was back on track.

Following his final pass, Amhara walked to the water vessel and dipped himself a drink. Kandake and Ezena reached him as he was toweling off.

"You did well," Ezena said. "I am sure you will make your rank."

"I wish I were as confident about that as you," Amhara said. "I fumbled the footwork and had to devise a different follow-through on that last pass."

"But is that not the reason for practicing? It is as Uncle Dakká says, no battle can be completely predicted. We learn our passes and moves so that we are prepared for any possibility." Kandake offered him another drink of water. "How soon will you know the outcome of the assessment?"

"Prince Dakká said that I will be told the results in the morning." He twisted the moisture from the bit of toweling he had used to wipe his arms and neck. He ran it over his face. "Right now all I want to do is find something to eat."

"I brought food with me," Ezena said, handing him the parcel she carried. "King Amani has permitted Kandake to journey with us to Aksum for grandmother."

"Is the king aware that I am traveling with you?" he asked, looking at Kandake. "I am one of her suitors."

"He knows," Kandake said. "And because you are going, I must bring along an elder."

The trio walked to their respective homes for evening meal. Kandake had promised to dine with her grandmother and headed toward her rooms. When she arrived, Great Mother was waiting for her. Several of the small tabletops were filled with dishes that were favorites of them both. Kandake bowed, honoring her grandmother.

"How does it feel to no longer be responsible for an entire kingdom?" Great Mother asked. She waved her granddaughter to the seat across from her.

"Relieved, Great Mother. It is a pleasure to have Father back on the throne." Kandake divided a piece of bread, offering her grandmother the larger portion. "It is helpful to know what awaits me, but it is a relief that it is not yet my rule."

Her grandmother smiled and nodded. "How are things progressing with your suitors? Has any one of them stood out that would cause you to choose him?"

"It is too early to tell." *But I know that it will be Amhara.*

"What about that young warrior you are so fond of? Would you not choose him?"

"I would, Great Mother," Kandake tried to hide the smile that the thought of choosing Amhara brought to her lips. "But it is not time for me to choose, yet."

"Your friend, Ezena, has chosen and set a date for her marriage ceremony. She is not that much older than you."

"It is true, Ezena is only a little more than one year my senior. Marriage is something she is ready for. I do not believe that I am." Kandake raced through her mind for a way to change the subject. *I enjoy his company. I even enjoy watching the way his muscles move beneath his skin when he works. But marriage is more than I want right now.*

"Ezena is traveling to Aksum to bring her grandmother here for the ceremony. Father is allowing me to travel with her."

"I remember her grandmother, Makeda," Great Mother said. A faraway look came into her eyes. "We were young girls together." She picked up a lump of cheese and bit into it. "I would like to see her again. I remember the things we would do to confound the young men who thought we should drop at their feet just because they were interested in us." She chuckled. "I would like to see what has become of some of them."

Kandake seized the opportunity. "Would you care to journey with us?"

"You would not want an old woman in your party. You would have to travel at a slower pace than you would like. I am no longer up to riding through the night."

"It would be no trouble, Great Mother. With Ezena's grandmother along, we had planned to make more rest periods than the usual."

"That pace would only be necessary for your return to Nubia. There is no reason your journey to Aksum would need to…." Great Mother stared into Kandake's face. "What is the real reason you would have me along? Would it have anything to do with a certain young warrior?"

_38_

Kandake held her grandmother's gaze, not sure of what to say. "Amhara will be traveling with Ezena. Father says I must either bring added warriors to post shield or ask an elder to accompany us."

"I see."

"I thought to ask you, and now I find that you know Ezena's grandmother. It would be an opportunity to visit your friend and help me. Please?"

"Why would you not take the warriors?"

"For two reasons. The first would be to protect Nubia. King Zoskales may misunderstand our presence and interpret it as an attack. And the second reason…." Kandake looked anywhere but at her grandmother. She smoothed her braids. She nibbled on a piece of bread. *Kandake, what is wrong with you? Just say it.* She took in a breath.

"If warriors were there to post shield, every conversation with Amhara would be monitored. He is one of my suitors, but we are still friends. I have always enjoyed his company and conversation."

Great Mother studied Kandake's face and said nothing for what felt like the length of time it would take to travel to Aksum. "I believe it would be nice to visit with Makeda and some of our old friends."

"Thank you Great Mother." Kandake relaxed and released the breath she had been holding. "I will help you pack whatever you wish to carry."

"I will hold you to that promise," she said, grinning at her granddaughter.

A few days later, Kandake and Natasen were piling all of the things their grandmother wished to take to her friend, Makeda, in Aksum.

"If you promised to help Great Mother pack," Natasen said, blowing out a weary breath. "Why am I doing the heavy lifting?"

"Because you are my brother and you love me." Kandake made a face, swatted his arm, and took off running. Natasen was within two steps of catching her when they skidded to a stop in front of their father.

"Prince Natasen! Princess Kandake! Is this how you plan to represent the kingdom while you are away?" King Amani said. He stood with his arms folded across his chest. A stern look pulled at his face.

Kandake would have been concerned had it not been for the grin tugging at the corner of his mouth.

"My King, we were just practicing our…uh...uh," Natasen stammered.

"Our chase and stop," Kandake added. "It is quite a valuable skill when chasing the enemy should he turn on you suddenly."

"Yes, My King…our chase and stop." Natasen nodded his head with great vigor.

"I see," King Amani said. His stared at Kandake, then slid his gaze to her brother. After a beat, the three burst into laughter. "And I am certain that this is a skill that must be practiced within the palace.

"Great Mother asked me to tell you that she has a few more things that need to go into the wagon."

"Yes, Father," Natasen said, rubbing his back. "Thank you."

They walked through the passageway to Great Mother's rooms.

"Good, you are both here," she said. "I need this last little bit to go into the wagon." She indicated the towering pile of things against the wall.

Kandake and Natasen loaded their arms with their grandmother's parcels.

"Great Mother, you are planning to return with us, are you not?" Natasen asked.

"Yes, I am," she said looking around the room as if she were searching for something else to pack. "Why do you ask?'

"It just seems like you are taking more than for a short visit."

She chuckled and shooed them on to the wagon with her things.

Once out of earshot Natasen said, "Tell me again why we are doing the loading and not one of the servants?"

"Because I promised to help her pack," Kandake said. Her voice reflected his sentiments. "When I said I would help her I had no idea she meant that I would be moving and arranging all of her belongings."

"Finally, we are at the end." Natasen grunted as he placed the last of Great Mother's bundles within the wagon. "From the looks of this, we will need an extra wagon when we return."

"Most of these are gifts for her friends in Aksum. We should have plenty of space on the return trip."

'Not if great Mother's friends are as generous as she is."

By late morning, everyone and all of their baggage was stowed away. With Great Mother's things, the gifts Ezena was taking to her aunt and grandmother, and those items belonging to the other travelers, there were two wagonsful. Sturdy oxen pulled them, with two servants driving each wagon. Great Mother chose to ride her horse for the beginning of the journey.

Amhara took turns with Natasen riding scout for the small party. Ezena and Kandake flanked either side of the wagons, and Shen brought up the rear. Great Mother alternated riding next to Kandake or Ezena.

"This journey will give me an opportunity to get to know that young man," Great Mother said.

Kandake followed her gaze toward Amhara's back as he rode at the head of the troop—the muscles beneath the skin bunched and released with the sway of his horse. She made an adjustment to her breastplate and corrected the drape of her quiver.

"His back is strong," her grandmother said, approval wrapping her words.

"It is," Kandake agreed. A smile tugged at the corners of her mouth.

"What has having this young warrior as a suitor taught you about him?"

Kandake snatched her mind from Amhara's back to answer her grandmother's question. "I already knew him to be a good friend," she began. She swatted at an insect flying around her eyes. "What stands out to me most is his willingness to work hard for what is important to him. He drove himself, practicing at every opportunity for his assessment to journeyman. He labored until every move was flawless."

She watched him for a moment. "It is not only his skills as a warrior, he approaches everything like that. He has a cow that will soon be ready to calf. Amhara sees to it that she has enough grass to eat and brings her drink instead of walking her to the watering hole. He keeps track of the direction of the breeze coming across the Nile. This is to decide which way the windows and doors should face to cool the house that he will build. All of this study and planning is before he has even bought the land." She nodded to herself. "He works hard, even in his plans."

Natasen returned. He brought his horse alongside his sister's. "There is a place up ahead that is suitable for our camp tonight."

"Is it far?" Great Mother asked, shifting in her saddle.

"No, Great Mother, we will be there soon."

"Good." Again, she changed positions.

"If you are tired, Great Mother," Kandake said. "There is a seat for you in the first wagon." Her grandmother declined the offer and continued on horseback.

Before long, the party reached the clearing Natasen indicated for their first night. Servants fed and watered the horses and oxen. Ezena and Amhara prepared the meal. While they ate, watches were assigned for the night. Kandake and Shen took their turns first. She stood guard just outside the camp while Shen patrolled the perimeter.

Completing his first circuit, Shen came to stand next to her. "Princess Kandake, how is it that we are traveling to the home of that…that…." He struggled for a word in the Nubian language. Failing to find one, he resorted to his own tongue.

She had no idea what the word meant, but read its meaning in his tone. "We are going because Ezena is my friend and it is my duty to support her."

"Are you not concerned that the prince of Aksum will cause you trouble?"

I would not be if you all would not continue to remind me.

39

That was the second time someone she respected warned her about her journey to Aksum. Kandake had dismissed Alara's warnings, not because he lacked wisdom, but more because he was her older brother and tended to be fairly protective. But now Shen was warning her.

He is a seasoned warrior. It is not like him to borrow danger without cause.

As the travelers set up camp, Kandake laid out her grandmother's bedding, making sure there were no stones beneath her blankets and stretching several layers of padding over the length of thick fleece. Next she erected an awning that would provide shade from the late afternoon and morning sun. Kandake then placed several dense pillows in a tight grouping for Great Mother to sit upon.

"Great Mother," Kandake said, handing her a dish of stew. "Alara and Shen have given me something to think about that causes me to question the wisdom of my journey to Aksum."

"Have they?" She spooned a bit of broth into her mouth, then set the dish aside to allow it to cool.

"Alara thinks I may be underestimating Prince Gadarat and the likelihood that he is holding onto his anger. Shen said something of the same." She dipped a corner of bread into her own bowl and chewed on it. "Why would the prince continue to be angry? I am giving Aksum back their mines without asking anything in return."

"And what about his loss of having you as his wife?"

"There was never any prospect of that. Even if he had maintained that marriage was a possibility, I have made it very clear that is not my wish."

"Precious Granddaughter, all men are not like those of Nubia." She shifted her position to look Kandake full in the face. "In our kingdom, men are taught from very young that it is the woman's choice and if she does not share his desire, he is free to seek elsewhere. That is not so in Aksum."

"In Aksum a man can continue his pursuit even after the woman has told him she is not interested?"

"In Aksum a woman has little say in who she weds." Great Mother took hold of Kandake's hand. "In Aksum, a woman's father arranges these things and a daughter must obey her father."

Kandake brooded over these words as she ate her meal. *If a woman is old enough to take a husband, is she not old enough to decide if she wants that husband?* "I know that I must honor my father, but if I am ready to start a family, should I not be able to choose?"

"You are thinking like a Nubian woman. In many kingdoms, women are not so respected. Does not Shen come from such a place?"

Kandake shifted her gaze to her new friend. She recalled his response at their initial meeting and her need to prove, to all in his company, her viability as a warrior. *Does he continue with those beliefs about women?* Shen's gaze met hers from across the camp. He smiled, bowed his head in a show of respect.

Her eyes focused upon Amhara. *He would never assume that I am weak. Amhara looks for my strength and encourages it. A marriage with such a man would be pleasure, our children would add to the kingdom's power and wealth.*

Prince Gadarat came to mind, so did thoughts of what marriage with him would be like. The waning of the day's heat was not enough to explain the sudden chill that came over her.

"Are you ill?" Great Mother asked. She reached out to Kandake.

"I am fine. What you said about the fathers of Aksum, could a father force a marriage if the woman believed the proposed husband to be a cruel man?"

"That would depend on the father, but it could happen."

Kandake thought of the blessings of being born in Nubia, but Great Mother had been born in Aksum.

"Your marriage to my grandfather, was that of your choosing?"

"Your grandfather was a wise man. I was visiting family in Nubia. He asked my father if he could present himself. Of course, my father said that was not necessary. Naqa said he would have it no other way and that a woman worthy of being queen was intelligent enough to make her own choice."

Kandake gathered her eating utensils, and her grandmother's, to clean them. She mulled over Great Mother's words as she rubbed the bowls with grit from the ground. Once cleaned of the remnants of their meal, she rinsed, dried, and packed the dishes away.

"Walk with me," Great Mother said, rising from the ground. "I need to shake out my bones."

The two women circled a wide perimeter of the camp. Shen followed them as protection. He maintained a respectful distance so as not to intrude upon their conversation.

"Great Mother, I am going into Aksum with two purposes. The main reason is to accompany Ezena to bring her grandmother back to Nubia for Ezena's marriage ceremony. The other is to present this document to King Zoskales transferring the mines to Aksum. I am Nubia's official representative in this."

Her grandmother reached out to a nearby bush, snagged one of its leaves and broke it, releasing its aromatic oils. "Umm, delicious." She rubbed a bit of the plant's oil into the skin of her shoulders.

"I am thinking that Prince Gadarat is likely still angry about my not choosing him, but I am not certain that he is selfish enough to put his disappointments ahead of his kingdom's needs. What do you think?"

"It is not important what I think," Great Mother said. "What matters is how you plan to proceed."

Kandake was caught up in quiet thought for the remainder of their circuit. *Prince Gadarat has shown himself to be a petty, spiteful man.*

40

Kandake laid out her sleeping mat next to her grandmother's. She studied Great Mother's face. The rich dark skin shone like polished ebony, not marked by age or disease. Words of encouragement and praise had always come from those full lips. Tight coils of her hair sparkled in the moonlight. *You are as beautiful as you are wise. I will give great thought as to how I enter Aksum. As things are, neither King Zoskales, nor his son, will be very pleased about my arrival.*

The morning sun found Kandake giving instructions to the servants. "You are to ride ahead of the party and announce our arrival." She pressed several small rings of gold into the man's hand. "Tell the king of Aksum that I come to visit the family of a dear friend, but that I will pay my respects to him before doing so. Inform him that I will arrive before evening meal." After she sent the servant away, she called the remainder of the party together.

"We will arrive in Aksum before the sun sets. I may not be as welcome as some of you."

"The prince may not be eager to see you, but he would not dare harm you," Natasen said. "I will make sure of that." He placed his hands upon his hips and his palm settled over the hilt of his knife.

"That is why you are not going with me." She held up her hand forestalling his complaint. "You will travel with Ezena and Amhara to the house of their grandmother and wait for me there."

"If Natasen is not going," Amhara said. "At least allow me to attend you. I do not trust these Aksumites!"

"An even greater reason for you to be elsewhere." Kandake stared at him until he agreed. "I am taking Great Mother with me and Shen will act as guard. He is not of Nubia. They will be less likely to feel threatened by his presence."

"What if—"

"If there is a problem, it is better that you are not with me. It leaves you free to come to my aid or go home to get help."

Late that afternoon they arrived in Aksum. Kandake noted the absence of the lush, green grasses of Nubia as this kingdom being further from the Nile River, but the people appeared to be healthy and strong. Even if King Zoskales was the scoundrel her father said, it appeared he treated his people well.

Kandake and Great Mother, accompanied by Shen, broke away from the rest of the party and went straight to the palace. At the entrance to the throne room her presence was announced and she was allowed an audience before King Zoskales.

"Princess Kandake," King Zoskales said, "It is good to see you." The king stood on the dais. Prince Gadarat stood to his right, arms folded across his chest, a sneer pasted to his face.

Kandake dipped a knee in respect for the man's position. "I have come to this kingdom to accompany a friend in preparation for her marriage ceremony. King Amani asked that I represent him while I am here."

"And you have brought home the woman of beauty my father desired." He left the dais to stand in front of Great Mother. "Zaria, it is a pity my father did not live to see the beauty you have become."

He turned his attention upon Kandake. "It is easy to see where this young beauty gets hers."

Kandake looked from King Zoskales to Prince Gadarat. *The son is definitely like the father!* She saw something flash in her grandmother's eyes, but couldn't read it. Something was not right. She read tension in Great Mother's body. She focused her attention on the king.

"How is your father?" King Zoskales asked. "He is well, I trust?"

"He is." Kandake scrutinized the man. She detected something in his manner. *What are you after?*

"It is a pity the prince could not have been more of a help to you during your father's illness." He glanced over his shoulder toward his son. "Prince Gadarat is still quite taken with you and hopes you will reconsider his offer."

Her body stiffened. Anger flared. She sucked in a hasty breath to respond, but reconsidered her words. "It is as I told the prince." She managed to mold her lips into a smile, softened her voice. "I am not ready to be wife to any man. I still have much to learn."

Out of the corner of her eye, she saw the hint of a grin on her grandmother's face.

"Now I understand your grandmother's presence. A young, unmarried woman of your beauty must be attended," he shifted his gaze to Shen, "and safeguarded. I see Zaria remembers the customs and ways of her home."

41

"Thank you, Great Mother," Kandake said, urging Strong Shadow to a swifter pace along the road. "If you had not told King Zoskales that we had promised to officiate the beginning of Ezena's marriage celebration, I believe we would have been obligated to stay the night in the palace."

"It did seem that way." Great Mother led the way. "It is also to our benefit that Ezena's grandmother is from a very influential family in Aksum." They turned onto an area of land where a sizeable herd of goats and many cows grazed. A generous porch opened onto the yard, welcoming them. Servants met them with vessels of cool water. Great Mother slid her gaze over the surrounding land. "Very little has changed over the years."

"Zaria!" A strong, rich voice called from the doorway. It was followed by a woman of Great Mother's years. Her smooth skin stretched over her face and body of soft ample curves. Kandake stared at the woman. It was like looking at Ezena many years from today, older, but just as lovely. "Ezena said you had come." She crushed Great Mother in a warm embrace.

She climbed down the steps with a strength and energy that belied the years her white hair attested to. "If I am looking upon the future queen of Nubia, it is hard to believe I am not looking at the queen of years gone by." Kandake dropped to her knees, offering her grandmother's friend great respect. "I would know your granddaughter anywhere." She kissed the top of Kandake's head.

Once they were shown their sleeping quarters, Kandake unpacked the gifts she had brought. After the evening meal, she placed one at the feet of Ezena's aunt and one at the feet of Great Mother's friend. She lowered herself to her knees facing Ezena's grandmother only slightly more than she did the aunt. "Thank you for welcoming me into your home. May your god keep your tables heavy with food, your pastures green with grass, and the ground beaten with the hooves of large herds."

"Thank you for your blessing, Kandake, granddaughter of my dear friend." She accepted her gift, a large bowl of the purest frankincense.

Kandake turned to face Ezena's aunt. "Thank you for the meal you have provided. May the laughter of children fill your house to over-flowing, may your breasts remain heavy with milk, and your children grow as the ebony, tall and strong."

"Thank you for your blessing, beloved friend of my sister's child."

Kandake stacked several bolts of fine linen into her arms. Nubian artisans had dyed each length of fabric a different rich color.

Music and laughter filled the remainder of the evening. Kandake listened as the grandmothers shared tales from their youth. Of particular interest was the story of how Great Mother managed to marry Kandake's grandfather instead of the father of King Zoskales. It was easy to understand the man's disappointment, but to expect the marriage to be stopped just because he made his desires known? It seemed that Prince Gadarat's arrogance was a family trait that passed through many generations.

The following morning greeted Kandake with an invitation to spend the day in the palace of Aksum.

"I do not believe this is a good idea, Kandake," Great Mother said. "King Zoskales is very much like his father, a man who believes the world is there to serve him and should be grateful for the opportunity."

"It is necessary that I meet with this king. If I do this now, I will be free to spend the rest of my time here with my friends." She adjusted her skirt, insuring the fabric draping from her hip covered the knife she wore next to her skin. Her torso, oiled to the finish of polished ebony. At her collar bone, she draped the

Nubian-fashioned double strand of beads, alternating calcite and carnelian. "Father asked that I deliver this." Kandake held out the leather-bound packet of papyrus sheets. She fastened on the golden armband that bore a large lapis stone, signifying an official representative of the kingdom of Nubia.

"If you will not permit me to accompany you, take Natasen with you."

"It is important that you remain with your friend, Great Mother. It has been many years since you have had an opportunity to visit. I will have Shen with me." She kissed the cheek of her grandmother. "I have Shen's strong arm to hold anyone off and Strong Shadow's swift feet should I need to leave quickly."

"I do not like this, granddaughter."

"I will be fine." Kandake walked out of the room. Shen met her at the bottom of the steps holding the reins of both of their horses. She vaulted to her mount's back, turned his head, and rode toward the palace.

"It is a pleasure to have your company, Princess Kandake," King Zoskales said. "It was unfortunate that I had to leave Nubia so soon that we had not had the opportunity to become better acquainted. I understand that your father fell ill soon after my departure."

"He is well, now. Thank you for your concern," Kandake said.

"I am certain that your father's illness weighed heavily upon you. His recovery must be a great relief."

I do not know where you are going with this conversation. What I have learned of you tells me that it cannot be good. "The citizens of Nubia celebrate King Amani's good health."

"Of this I am certain," he said. Zoskales led Kandake to an area adjoining the throne room. He offered her a seat.

She sat in the chair across the table from him. Shen took up a position to the side of her, a few steps to her rear.

"Would you care for refreshment?" The king called a servant over.

"A cool drink of water would be welcome," she said.

"Water would be fine for your man," he indicated Shen, "but I understand that you favor the juice of pomegranates." He turned to instruct the servant.

"Water would be best for both of us," she said, adding a ring of authority to her voice.

"Make it as the princess says," King Zoskales ordered. "My son told me you preferred having things your way."

42

Kandake lifted the vessel to her mouth. She sipped at its contents and set it back on the table. "I do not know your purpose for inviting me, but I will use this opportunity to discuss my father's business with you." She placed the leather-bound sheaf onto the table. "The matter of the mines must be settled."

"You are correct. That is not the reason for my invitation. We can discuss this," he waved a dismissive hand over the packet, "at a later time. I would like to discuss Prince Gadarat."

That arrogant shoat! Kandake ground her teeth. *There is nothing for us to speak of.* She worked at maintaining a pleasant expression upon her face. "Your son?"

"That is the issue." He leaned forward, locked his gaze with hers. "Prince Gadarat is my first son, and as such, one day this kingdom will be his." He took a long drink of his beverage. "And you will have Nubia."

"No person HAS Nubia. Nubia is a kingdom of people—strong people. I *serve* Nubia."

"Yes, yes, but a marriage between you and the prince would bring the two kingdoms together— making them a stronger, greater people."

Kandake sent herself through one of the warrior exercises—one meant to calm the mind and the spirit. She waited for it to take effect before she spoke. "King Zoskales," she emphasized his title. "As King Amani explained," she emphasized her father's title, also. "A Nubian woman takes a husband WHEN she has decided, WHOM she has decided. It is not the time, nor have I chosen."

Zoskales sat back in his chair. He scrutinized Kandake's face. Silence surrounded them.

The meat in this kingdom must be rancid, filled with worms. Why else would these two continue to hold onto what will NEVER be?

Laughter burst from King Zoskales. "Now I understand. You are just like my son!"

Kandake's jaw dropped. She felt her eyes must be bulging from her head.

"Neither of you wishes to be tied to another at this time. Just like him, you wish time to sample life!" He laughed louder. "What was I thinking?" He smacked his forehead. "You have just reached the age of womanhood. Of course. You want to know what men are like before you take Prince Gadarat." He continued to laugh until tears of mirth trickled down his cheeks.

Shen move to her side. She was sure he was responding to the insult this king delivered. If Nubia would not pay the price, she would have given him her leave to attack this offensive, yipping hyena. She lifted a hand to stop him.

"That is the reason you bring the young warrior with you—to indulge your pleasures away from the eyes of your people. A very wise move." He wiped the tears with his sleeve. "Now I understand the reason you bring Zaria with you. She would understand the need to do this here, away from the watchfulness of your kingdom and so that my son could understand."

*Is that what you think of Nubia's crown? You think that I would dishonor my kingdom in this way. That I would bring shame to my father…*Kandake seethed…*to myself!* Anger warred with rage. She stood—snatched the bundled pages from the table.

"No, no," King Zoskales stood. His body quaked with his amusement. "We cannot discuss business today. I must go have a talk with the prince. He is under the impression that you prefer that warrior to him." He guffawed. "Come back tomorrow. We will deal with it then."

Kandake's eyes bored holes into the man's back as he left the room.

"Princess Kandake, you should have allowed me to silence him," Shen said, mounting his horse outside the palace.

"This is neither the time nor the place. Nubia will not go to war because of one foolish, ill-mannered man." The sharp dig of her heels into the sides of Strong Shadow belied her pretense at calm. She rode him hard all the way back to the home of Ezena's grandmother.

A flurry of activity met Kandake as she pulled the horse to a stop in front of the main house. She dismounted. In one long stride, she climbed the stairs and entered the house. Shen followed close behind. The servants greeted her, but none would look her in the eye. She found Great Mother agitated, holding and comforting her old friend.

"What has happened?" she asked a nearby servant.

"They have taken them," Ezena answered, coming into the room. Her filled quiver hung at her back. She paused long enough to fasten her bow string. "I am going to bring them back."

"Bring who back? Who was taken? What happened?"

"While you were gone, Prince Gadarat, and some of his men, came to arrest Amhara," Great Mother said.

"Arrest Amhara? For what?" Kandake looked from her grandmother to her friend.

"The prince accused Amhara of spying for Nubia." Ezena tied her sling to her hip.

"That is ridiculous! We are here openly."

"True, and when they tried to take him, Natasen stepped in. They arrested him, too." Great Mother said, trying to coax her friend to sip the water the servant had brought.

"Prince Gadarat arrested Amhara AND Natasen?" Kandake stripped the band from her arm, tossed the papers to the floor. "Give me a moment to change," she said to Ezena. "I am going with you!"

43

In the small amount of time it took Great Mother to catch up with her granddaughter, Kandake had already changed her skirt, tied a knife to one hip, her sling to the other, and was fastening her breastplate into place.

"That horse's hind-end has gone too far." Kandake snatched up her bow. "He knows that Amhara is no spy, and for what reason has he arrested my brother?"

"To goad you into this." Great Mother pointed at Kandake's breastplate and weapons.

"Am I to stand here and allow Prince Gadarat to …?" She waved her free hand around in the air searching for the word she wanted.

"You must not do this," her grandmother pleaded. "Attacking the palace means war."

"I am not attacking Aksum, I am going to get my brother back."

"Princess Kandake, you know there is more to it than that."

"Great Mother, when Alara was missing, both Ezena and Amhara went with me to rescue him. I never asked them to go. They insisted. How could I do less now?"

Kandake returned to the room where she had left her friend's grandmother. Ezena looked every bit the Nubian warrior. Shen stood beside her, battle ready.

"Good," Kandake said. "We will leave."

"Before you leave, you must hear me." Ezena's grandmother said. "I want my grandson back, but we must find another way."

"I am a warrior," Ezena said. "There is no other way. We all know that Amhara is no spy, including Prince Gadarat! He is angry because Kandake has refused to marry him and he believes that Amhara is the reason."

Kandake knelt before the older woman. "What my friend says is true. I have refused marriage with Aksum's prince, but Amhara is not the only reason. I am not ready to take a husband and if I were, Prince Gadarat would not be my choice. I do not wish to bring problems between Aksum and Nubia, but I will not allow Amhara, or Natasen, to be harmed because of me."

"My granddaughter has told me of this. But we who are old have learned to look through to the next season." She took hold of Kandake's hand, pulled her to the seat beside her. "Princess Kandake, you are a guest here in Aksum. You have little understanding of the dealings between the prince and his father. King Zoskales is not an evil man."

Kandake opened her mouth to disagree, but Ezena's grandmother interrupted.

"Please, hear me out," she said. "King Zoskales is not always the most honest in his business dealings with the surrounding kingdoms, but his intensions are good. He wants what is best for Aksum and he thinks greater wealth will insure this. His son is different.

"The prince has lived knowing that he will one day rule this kingdom. He takes this to mean that his word is already law and that the things he does are within that law. His father does not always agree. Go to his father."

"What Makeda says is true." Great Mother sat next to Kandake on the long bench. "If you take this matter to the father, he will have to address the actions of his son."

"And if the father agrees with the son?" Kandake asked.

"Then you have this option waiting for you." Ezena's grandmother placed her hand upon Kandake's bow.

Kandake looked to Ezena.

"We can try talking with the king first, but…." Ezena left the sentence hanging.

Kandake turned toward Shen. "Princess Kandake, I will follow you, whatever path you choose."

"I will attempt to reason with the king and see if he is better than the son, as you say," she assured her grandmother's friend. "I will go to the palace as the princess of Nubia, but if he does not release them, I will return to face them as a Nubian warrior."

44

A servant ushered Kandake into the throne room of Aksum. King Zoskales sat on his throne, Prince Gadarat stood at his right hand. She lowered herself in respect.

"King Zoskales, there has been an insult made to Nubia and Aksum. My brother, Prince Natasen of Nubia, and my friend Amhara, a Nubian warrior, have been taken and held by this kingdom. Please release them."

"I am not aware of Nubia being taken." He looked at his son. His expression conveyed displeasure as it asked a question.

"The one she claims as a warrior of Nubia was taken because of crimes against Aksum and her brother attacked those sent to arrest the warrior," Gadarat said, his voice filled with accusation.

"King Zoskales, the prince knows there were no crimes committed. The warrior came to escort his grandmother to Nubia to attend the marriage ceremony of a family member." Though she spoke to Zoskales, Kandake's glowered at his son.

"Father, this woman has come to Aksum to see what other lands she will steal for Nubia. And since her agent was discovered, she hides the truth for that man."

"King Zoskales, now the prince insults me. Nubia has no interest in the holdings of Aksum. I have stated the occasion of my presence in this kingdom."

"She lies! I told you how she deceived me. She accepted me as her suitor only to gain control of our mines." Prince Gadarat strode from his place next to his father on the dais to stand in front of Kandake. "Look at you, dressed as a woman. Something you know nothing of. If it were left to me, I would teach you the meaning of your place." He spat at her feet.

"I remember, Prince Gadarat," Kandake said, struggling to hold onto any calm she had ever felt. "You attempted to instruct me in knowing my place not long ago, but I recall that lesson did not turn out so well." The sound of a smothered chuckle reminded her of his presence.

"King Zoskales," Kandake said, not breaking the locked gaze she held with the prince. "In Nubia, if a man commits a crime and is arrested, the one attempting to free him by force receives twice the punishment of the original crime. I request that you would allow me to see both men to make certain neither has been harmed, since both are innocent."

"They are both guilty and neither will be released," Prince Gadarat said through clenched teeth.

Kandake narrowed her eyes. "I am addressing the king."

"I see no problem in Princess Kandake visiting the prisoners." King Zoskales said. He put emphasis on her title.

"Let her go to them," the prince said. "But her armed man remains here."

Kandake was taken to the guarded structure where Natasen and Amhara were held. Light was dim inside the small, windowless room. It stank of past tenants relieving themselves without benefit of a service pot. Rage stabbed again at Kandake's heart.

"Are you staying the night?" Natasen asked, making a joke of the situation. "We could ask for more straw, but I think there is a shortage within the kingdom. This has not been changed recently."

"I do not believe that I will," Kandake said. "This room is small and with the way you thrash about in your sleep, I would be pummeled." She squatted between the two and looked them over. "Are you badly injured?"

"The bruises are nothing, but my arms ache from the bindings," Natasen said.

"That is because one of them beat me after I was tied," Amhara added. "Prince Natasen broke his bonds and beat him. I fear there will be damage to his hands, the leathers that bind them are much too tight."

"How often do they check you?" Kandake asked.

"No one has checked since we were placed in here, but I am sure they will once you have left."

"Listen to me," Kandake said. "I will do what I can to have the king release you, but if I cannot, I will come back and do it myself. I know why you are here and I blame myself. It is my responsibility to see that you are free."

She unfastened the thong that held her braids. "I want this back," she told Amhara. She slid the bronze piece he had given her along the ground and slipped it beneath his thigh. "I am leaving now. After they have confirmed that I have not loosed you, cut Natasen free." She stood, rearranged her hair and called for the guards.

Kandake returned to the throne room to collect Shen.

"I trust that you found them in good condition?" King Zoskales asked.

"There were no serious injuries, but I still require they be released."

"Then return our property to Aksum," the prince demanded. "Give us what you have stolen and we may return what is yours."

"Nubia does not barter for its citizens. You will return them because you have no right to hold them." She faced Prince Gadarat. "Coming here, it had been my intention to gift Aksum the mines that lie south of Nubia's borders—a gift for a friend. Your actions have brought that friendship into question." She addressed

King Zoskales. "Is Aksum a friend of Nubia or is this kingdom Nubia's enemy?"

45

"Are you threatening this kingdom?" Prince Gadarat moved into her line of sight. "Should Aksum be preparing for war?"

"There has been no talk of war," King Zoskales said, rising from his throne. "Princess Kandake has made no mention of it." He directed his attention toward Kandake. "Please excuse the prince. It is his love for this kingdom that raises such passion within him."

"Father, do you fear her father so much that you would—"

"My son, this is not the place for this conversation," the king interrupted. "It has been a long day and I am sure that the princess requires food and rest."

"What I require is the release of my brother, and my friend," Kandake said.

"Do you see? She calls that enemy her friend," Prince Gadarat argued. "What else do you need to hear, Father?"

"I need to hear that evening meal has been prepared. We will continue after we have eaten."

"King Zoskales, please understand the freedom of Nubian citizens is more important to me than food."

The king walked toward the doorway and beckoned that Kandake follow. The area they entered had a long table set along the far wall. Its top was covered with platters of meats, cheeses, fruits and bread. A servant directed Kandake to a low table set upon a rug woven in bright colors. Coordinating pillows were strewn about it.

Once she had been seated, a plate filled with slices of roasted meats: wild pig, sheep, and goat, fresh baked bread, and portions of fruit was placed before her. Another servant filled a small bowl with pomegranate juice and another with water and set those beside Kandake's plate. A dish of brined olives and nuts was placed within her reach.

"My son tells me that these are your favorites," King Zoskales said. "Please enjoy."

Prince Gadarat sat on the floor across from Kandake.

"Please excuse me," King Zoskales said. "I have become accustomed to taking evening meal in the night air, alone."

"King Zoskales," Kandake said, rising from the table. "We must speak."

"We will, after you have taken refreshment. Would you have your father believe that I neglected his daughter?" He walked from the room without a backward glance. She stared after him.

Kandake stared at the plate. *I will not be put off!* She pushed her plate away.

"You may as well eat," Prince Gadarat said. "He will not speak with either of us until he has eaten and believes we have ironed out our differences." He slid her plate back in place.

Prince Gadarat took a huge bite of the meat. The way he tore into it led Kandake to believe he was not pleased either. The meal progressed in silence. *What can his father hope to gain from this meal? It certainly will not be a daughter—at least not me!*

"My father attempted to explain your presence in Aksum, especially with that warrior. But I do not believe him."

"You will have to believe what you will. I have given you my reason for being here." Kandake sipped her juice.

"I cannot say I know what brought you here, but I know you. You will not leave without them." He jerked his head in the direction Natasen and Amhara were being held. "And I will not release them until I have what I desire."

Kandake pushed her plate aside, once more. She propped her elbows on the table, blocking the dish's return and spoke to the prince over her clasped fingers in low menacing tones. "I have no care for what you desire or what pleases you. My only interest in Aksum, at this point, is the release of Nubian citizens.

Holding them without just cause is an act of war. Are you prepared for that?" She leaned away from the table staring him straight in the eyes, without waver.

"Do not press me, woman. This is not Nubia."

"I have completed my meal." Kandake stood with slow, deliberate movement. "Please tell King Zoskales that I will speak with him once he has finished." She moved toward the exit.

"You will not leave this room until I say."

"Prince Gadarat," Kandake kept her back to him, "please give the king my message." She walked through the doorway. Shen followed. The loud noise of crashing dishes and platters came from the room she had just left.

Kandake stood out in the palace courtyard breathing in the night's warm, scented air. The stars overhead winked at her as if they shared the pleasure she took in leaving the prince in that manner.

"It is not my place to criticize your actions, Princess Kandake," Shen said. "But do you think it wise to anger the prince like that while he holds my friends?"

"You are correct, Shen. That was not the wisest thing to do, but it felt so good." She threw her arms over her head as if freeing herself from some heavy burden.

Shen chuckled.

"Princess Kandake," a servant called, approached and dropped to one knee. "The king has sent you a message." He proffered a small strip of papyrus.

_46_

Kandake read the message. "What do you think of this?" She passed it to Shen.

He stared at the small sheet. It took him some time to decipher the unfamiliar language. "It says that you must visit your brother right now." He turned the paper over in his hands as if searching for more information. "This reads like a warning."

"That is how I read it. We had better hurry."

Kandake and Shen wound a path back through the palace, making their way to the small building in which Natasen and Amhara were being held.

"Where are the guards?" she asked.

Shen looked around them, peering into the shadows as if anticipating a trap. "I see no one."

Kandake laid her hand upon the latch of the door. "It is not locked." She pushed the door inward in tiny increments, assuming, at any moment, the wooden slab would be yanked from her grasp. It was not.

Inside, the room was dark. With little strain, she made out the figures of the two men where she expected them to be sitting. Not ready to trust that this was not some other method the prince had set to ensnare her, she allowed Shen to enter, then used her bodyweight to close and seal the door.

When her eyes adjusted to the dimness, she found herself staring into the faces of her brother and her suitor.

"What is happening?" Natasen asked. "There was some disturbance just outside and then nothing. Amhara was creeping to the door to find out, but heard you and moved back."

"I am not certain, but I believe we had better take advantage of whatever it is and leave."

"But how did the two of you get here?" Amhara asked, rising to his feet.

"We will talk later."

Shen cracked open the door to peek outside. "There are still no guards out there."

The four of them slipped from the building. In a low crouch, they made their way toward the stables.

"We will have to ride doubled," Kandake said. "We only have Strong Shadow and Shen's horse."

With no lack of speed, Shen and Natasen saddled the two horses. Each mounting one, they assisted another to ride with them and maneuvered the animals toward the nearest exit. They rode their mounts as hard as they dared—swift hooves eating up the distance back to Amhara's grandmother's home.

Kandake dismounted just as Strong Shadow reached the porch. "Have the horses watered and rubbed down. Prepare the wagons and animals to travel," she barked the orders at the nearest servant. "We return to Nubia immediately." She threw the remaining instructions over her shoulder as she walked through the door.

"You brought them back!" Great Mother snagged both of the young men in a tight embrace.

"How long will it take you to pack to leave?" Kandake asked her grandmother.

"I could be ready by early morning," she said. Great Mother looked to her friend. "Is that enough time for you, Makeda?" Her friend nodded.

"Then get as many servants as you need to help you. We need to leave before the moon reaches its height."

"Kandake, what is it?" Ezena's grandmother asked.

"I do not have time to explain. May I borrow your fastest horse?" She called one of the Nubian servants to her. "You must return to the kingdom with all the speed the horse will give you. Go straight to the palace. Tell my father I have need of Prince Dakká."

Every person in the room stared at Kandake. Their expressions said they were aware of the danger ahead—and that danger included the possibility of war.

47

"We need to get moving," Kandake said as Natasen and Shen loaded the last of the items into the wagons. She tested and adjusted the harnesses for each wagon. She directed the older women to begin the trek riding in the wagons, thinking it would be less arduous for them as they would be traveling throughout the night.

"This belongs to you," Amhara said. He unwrapped the thong of the bronze disk from his arm. "When I gifted you this, I had no idea you would need it so soon." He flashed her his ready smile and vaulted to the back of his horse.

"Kandake," her brother called to her, "Amhara will be riding ahead of us; he is the best at scouting a trail. I want you and Ezena to protect our flank. Shen and I will be at the rear. If we are attacked from behind, he and I can hold them off long enough for you to get to cover."

As Kandake listened, she admired the way her brother put to use the skills he was learning from their uncle. *Natasen will be a strong Prime Warrior. Again, I see the wisdom of Great Mother's choices.* She urged Strong Shadow forward to deliver his instructions to the others.

The wagons moved with as much speed as a yoke of oxen could provide. The promise of sunrise nibbled at the far horizon when Natasen called to her. Kandake dropped back to hear what he had to say.

"I hear rumbling." He directed his gaze toward the sky. "There is a clear view of the stars, so the sound can only by horses, driven hard. Tell Amhara we will need ground we can hold."

Kandake put her heels to Strong Shadow's sides. The horse leapt into full gallop. The wagons were only a blur as she passed.

"Amhara!" Kandake shouted. "Natasen says to find a place to stand."

The young warrior acknowledged her with a hand signal and urged his horse forward. Kandake dropped back to her flanking position and shared what was happening with Ezena and the others.

"Natasen has only heard the hoof beats of their horses, but it will not be long before we see them."

Ezena signaled her understanding.

"Great Mother," Kandake said, moving near to the wagon so her grandmother could hear. "We are being pursued. If there is trouble, the both of you will be mounted and Amhara will lead you to safety."

"I will not run and hide. I will remain with you."

"It was not a suggestion. Although I am no longer your queen, I need you to obey me in this. Once you are gone, we will hold them long enough for you to reach Nubia."

"We are not that far from the kingdom now. You need every warrior here with you. You need Amhara fighting alongside you, not guiding two old women across The Strand."

"It is better if we stay," Ezena's grandmother said. "Amhara's bow is needed. You would worry about our safety no matter where we were. If we stay, all you would need do is look in our direction to assure yourself we have come to no harm."

Kandake expelled an exasperated breath. "I am beginning to think Prince Gadarat has the wrong opinion of Aksumite women if the others are anything like these two." She turned Strong Shadow away from the side of the wagon. She shook her head at the sound of the elder women's giggles.

She trotted her horse back to Natasen's position far behind the last wagon.

"From the size of the dust cloud, I would say that the group following us may be at least ten horses." He looked to Shen for his opinion. The man nodded.

"I am certain that is the prince and his men," Kandake said.

"Amhara has found a defensible position for the wagons, just ahead," Ezena said, joining them. "He says that we should place them at the backside of that cluster over there." She pointed in the direction of a grouping of enormous boulders, varying in size and shape. "It will provide adequate cover for the wagons and at the same time allow us to move around without making us easy targets."

"Good," Natasen said. "Tell him to do it." Ezena pushed her horse into a dead run to get the information back to her cousin.

By the time the party of riders reached them, Kandake and the others were behind cover giving them the strategic positioning of being on higher ground. From her vantage point, Kandake saw Prince Gadarat accompanied by twelve Aksumite warriors. She stepped from behind a stone pillar.

"Prince Gadarat, why do you follow us? Is there something that you need?"

"You know why we are here," the prince barked from the back of his horse. "We have come for the prisoners your Scythian assassin removed from Aksum. Return them and you may go."

"Shen is not an assassin, he is a warrior. It was not he who freed my brother and friend, I did it. You had no right to hold them."

"Of course I had the right. They were spying against the kingdom. I demand that you return them or these warriors will take them from you."

"We are going to Nubia—all of us. If you have a lawful claim, you may present it to King Amani—in Nubia."

"Those are strong words for someone that has no way to support them. That line of rocks," he pointed toward the distance behind Kandake, "marks the boundary of your kingdom. That is a long way to travel and there is much that can happen between here and there."

"I could say the same of you, Prince Gadarat. You left the boundary to Aksum some distance back. Where we stand is at the center of the Strand of Nonaligned Ground. This land belongs to neither kingdom. If you attack us on this land there will be war between Aksum and Nubia."

"The boundary of Aksum extends as far as I say it does—including that patch of dirt you call a kingdom."

Rage flashed through Kandake. It saturated every muscle of her body. The tips of the fingers of her right hand ached for a bow string to pull. Her hip screamed to be relieved of the weight of her knife.

48

"Prince Gadarat of Aksum." Her body trembled with the effort restraint cost her as her feet carried her closer to him. "It is because of my love of Nubia that I do not rid the world of you."

She climbed down the last of the rocks. "I have ignored your insults. I have tolerated your arrogance. And when you did the unthinkable—capture my brother and my dear friend's cousin—I allowed my grandmother's wisdom to influence my action."

Kandake came to stand in front of him on level ground. "Behind me are two elders, one of Nubia and the other of Aksum. Good friends who have begun celebrating the marriage ceremony of a granddaughter. Our kingdoms have spent generations doing just this. What you are pushing here today will tarnish what should be the foundation of hope to come." She brought a soothing tone to her voice. "I ask you, do not taint the future of their marriage. Do not bring war to our homes."

"Finally, the humility that should come from a woman," Prince Gadarat said. The sneer on his face grew to a self-satisfied grin as he dropped from horseback. "You may ask me to grant this wish from your knees."

The prince turned toward the men behind him. A mirthless chuckle escaped his lips. Kandake had seen Gadarat do this once before. The last time he had responded in this way, he had taken her by surprise. Today there was nothing surprising in his behavior. The prince brought his right hand around to deliver Kandake a quick, tight slap, but she was prepared. His hand connected with air.

One step to her right and slightly back caused him to reach for her. She plowed her fist into the side of his head. It knocked him to the ground.

"What are you waiting for?" he said from his back. "Take her!"

The Aksumite warrior nearest Kandake moved to dismount. An arrow kicked up dust at his horse's forefoot.

"Get off of that horse and you are dead." Natasen's voice held the edge of cold, sharp iron. "Little sister, come back, no one will harm you."

"You heard my command! Take her!" Gadarat shouted, pushing himself to a seated position.

"My brother will kill him if he moves."

"He will do as I have commanded."

"Do you care so little for the life of your people?" She raised her eyes to the man on horseback. "Please do not move. This is not worth your life. There is no honor to be had in that death."

"Woman, shut your mouth! I am the man here." Gadarat reached out and grabbed Kandake's ankle and the waistband of her skirt. He yanked her to the ground next to him.

Kandake extended her left arm and struck, delivering the prince a powerful backhand blow to his nose.

"Augh!" The pain-filled cry burst from Gadarat's lips. He snatched a handful of Kandake's braids and pulled her backwards. Her head smacked the ground with a muffled thud. Gadarat's attempt to straddle her was deterred. Using as much force as she could muster, Kandake stamped the sole of her foot into his groin. She splayed her hands on his chest, and flipped him over her head. He slammed onto his back, raising a cloud of dust.

Kandake climbed to her feet. He came at her like a crazed beast. She dealt him a double-fisted blow to the side of his head. He went down and rolled to his back.

Kandake stepped one foot between his thighs with her heel dangerously close to the already injured intersection. She placed her other foot on his neck.

"I will not ask you to surrender," she breathed. "You would only lie." She stared into his face. Blood ran in rivulets from his nose. Twin daggers of hatred stabbed at her from his eyes. Her ears drummed from the pounding of her heart. *You deserve to die. Aksum would be better off without you. The world would be better off without you.*

Kandake felt the shift of balance between her feet. The knob within Gadarat's neck shivered and poked at the bottom of her foot. Every muscle, every desire begged her to shift her weight. All she had to do was add just a tiny bit of force…it would not take much at all.

WHAT ARE YOU DOING? THIS IS NOT WHO YOU ARE! THIS IS NOT THE QUEEN OF NUBIA!

Never removing her gaze from his, Kandake eased back the pressure of her foot. With great restraint and calculated effort she removed her foot completely and set it next to the other one with delicate care. She raised her eyes to see everyone watching her—Nubian and Aksumite alike.

Thunder rumbled from the ground beaten by the hooves of many horses. A contingent of Aksumite warriors on horseback, led by King Zoskales and his second son, came to a stop behind the warriors brought by Prince Gadarat. As if the timing had been orchestrated, at the same time a band of Nubian warriors, led by King Amani and Prince Dakká, halted behind Natasen and the other Nubians. Kandake could not say when those traveling with her had left their position on the rocks. Nor could she have said when the Aksumites accompanying Gadarat dismounted.

"She tried to kill me!" Prince Gadarat shouted, scrambling to his feet, screaming to his father and pointing at Kandake as she walked away from him. "Did you hear what I said? That graceless sow of Nubia tried to kill me!"

King Zoskales stared at his son, saying nothing. His expression exhibited harsh displeasure. Then he spoke. "I heard what you said."

"Will you do nothing?" Prince Gadarat asked, incredulous.

Again, his father's stony silence.

"No woman does this to the prince of Aksum and lives," Prince Gadarat growled. He charged at Kandake's back.

Kandake heard him coming. She spun around to meet him. She yanked her knife from its scabbard in a cross-reach with her left hand. This kept her right hand free to strike the prince or block his blow to her. She had no desire to inflict any serious injury.

He came at her so fast, she misjudged the distance between them. The sweep of her blade that was meant as a warning sliced the front of his thigh. Prince Gadarat screamed. He collapsed at the feet of Kandake.

NO! Her mind screamed, over and over.

Kandake bent to examine the fallen prince. An arrow protruded through the calf of Gadarat's right leg.

Immediately she looked to her brother and the Nubians standing near him. He shook his head in denial. Kandake shifted her gaze to the Aksumite warriors. The man on horseback nearest to King Zoskales was in the act of returning his bow to his back. The king dispatched two of his men to retrieve his son. They carried the prince to his horse and tied him into his saddle, giving little attention to bracing the leg with the arrow piercing it.

49

Kandake and Ezena sat beneath the shading boughs of an acacia tree not far from the palace in the safety of Nubia. The warm afternoon breeze wrapped around Kandake's skin like a familiar blanket. She stretched out on her belly watching the progress of an ant carrying a grain of something.

"Have you and Nateka decided where you will live?" Kandake blocked the path of another ant with a bit of rock. She watched the insect double back on its trail only to retrace its steps to the blockage. When the insect reached it, she whisked the stone away and placed a twig further along its route.

"There is a section of land that is perfect for building a house with room enough for an ironworks arrangement at the rear. He would like to take on an apprentice or two, someday."

"I am certain your mother will encourage that he add many rooms to the house for all of the children she is hoping you will have." Kandake ducked as Ezena swatted at her.

"There you are!" Tabiry said. Her words had the sound of accusation rather than discovery. "I have searched the entire kingdom, trying to find your hiding place."

"I am not hiding," Kandake said. "What have I done this time?" She rolled onto her side to sit up. She turned her giggle into a cough catching sight of the expression on Ezena's face.

"Do not pretend. You know what you did," Tabiry huffed with her hands on her hips. "And since you are no longer queen, I can tell you exactly what I think." She stood glaring at Kandake. "Well…I am waiting."

"Waiting for what?"

"I am waiting for you to explain to me why you thought it necessary to drag Prince Gadarat to the middle of the Strand and stab him with that?" She pointed to the knife at Kandake's hip.

"I did no such thing."

"Of course you did. You said so in Council this morning."

"I did not drag the prince anywhere. He followed me—no, I would say that he chased me and I did not stab him. My knife cut his thigh when he attacked me. And that was not intentional."

"Little sister, you cannot fool me. I know better than that. You are battle starved and will do anything to practice being a warrior." Tabiry's voice cracked. She stared at her sister. "You do not care if I never get married," she wailed. Tabiry collapsed into a crumpled pile at Kandake's feet. Ezena gave Kandake a questioning look as if asking if she should leave. Kandake shrugged her shoulders not knowing what would be best.

Kandake held her sister until her crying quieted. She wiped Tabiry's face with the tail of her own skirt. "What is this all about? You keep complaining that my actions are preventing you from choosing a husband and having your ceremony. Are you planning to choose?" She stared into her sister's eyes. "Tell me the truth."

"I am, but you and Father will laugh at me."

"We would never do such a thing. You are a Nubian woman, and that gives you freedom to choose which ever man pleases you. Do you fear that this man will not accept your choice?" Kandake felt the stirrings of protectiveness toward her sister.

"I am certain he will accept it, it is just that…." Her voice tapered off. Her gaze bounced between Kandake and Ezena.

"I will leave," Ezena said.

"You do not need to go. It concerns you as much as it does Kandake." She took a deep breath and let it out in a slow hiss. "It is that if Nubia goes to war with Aksum—" a tight shake of her head stopped Kandake when she opened her mouth to interrupt. "It is true. We could go to war. I heard Natasen's report. Aksum went too far—arresting our brother and her cousin, following you onto the Strand and attacking you there. Prince Gadarat ordered his man to 'take you.' You have every right to strike that kingdom. They have earned it. But if you do, the man I will choose will go with you. How can there be a marriage ceremony if you, Natasen, Uncle Dakká, and my chosen are away fighting a war?" Tears rolled from her eyes. She buried her face in her hands.

"Tabiry, I have said that I will not exercise that right. I could have killed the prince on the Strand. I had my foot on his neck. I wanted to end his life. But, I thought of you. I thought of your wanting to choose. I thought of the nieces and nephews that you will give me. I thought of how beautiful Nubia is and I could not do it."

She dried her sister's face—once more. "If ever there was a man who needed killing, it is Prince Gadarat, but his death is not worth losing all of this." She extended her hand to include the land surrounding them. "No, Princess Tabiry, there will be no war with Aksum."

_50_

Two days later, the day Ezena would marry
Nateka, Kandake sat behind Ezena, braiding the last
sections of her friend's hair. To the braid just behind
Ezena's right ear she tied a stone of lapis braced in
gold. "This jewel is to tell Nateka, and everyone else,
you are the dear friend of the queen."

She slathered oil infused with frankincense over
her friend's shoulders, massaged it into her skin, and
helped her to her feet. Kandake smoothed the fabric
wrapped around Ezena's hips. It was made of calf's
skin and decorated with clusters of beads. She checked
the knot that fastened it at her friend's side, just below
her waist. She then wrapped a braid of fine, gold wire

about her friend's waist. A clasp made of malachite and gold covered her navel.

Kandake stepped back from Ezena to admire her friend. She looked beautiful. The young women embraced as a knock sounded at the door.

"What do you want here?" Ezena's father asked the traditional question of the young man standing in the doorway.

"I have come for my wife," Nateka said. He wore a robe of fine linen. From the hips upward, the cloth had been dyed a bright yellow that rivaled the sun. It signified the hope of their lives together. Below the hips the fabric was dyed a brilliant blue-green representing the richness of the land supported by the waters of the Nile River. The kilt about his hips was the same vibrant blue-green of the robe. His chest was bare and the skin polished to the texture of burnished ebony, smooth and dark.

"This is for the honor you do me in raising such a woman." He placed a large sack in her father's hands. Poking out of the opening were items of hand-crafted iron, carved wood, smaller sealed sachets likely containing herbs, myrrh, incense, and other valuable commodities.

"How do I know that it is enough?" her father asked, hefting the bag.

"It could never be enough," Nateka answered, "but I promise my life's labor and strong shelter for as long as she will have me."

The traditional words spoken, Ezena's father took her hand and placed it into the hand of Nateka. She stepped over the threshold of her family's home and into the road next to the man she would marry. Together they walked, with friends and family following close behind, to the land where they would build their new home.

Along the way, Ezena's grandmother offered her words of wisdom about marriage and motherhood. Kandake offered her friend sips of water and morsels of food to symbolize her support of her friend and strength for Ezena's journey. On the other side, Kashta instructed his son in the responsibilities of a man caring for his family. Alara, his closest friend, promised to stand by him, assuring and encouraging Nateka that he would succeed in his every endeavor.

At last they arrived. A spacious tent had been erected as temporary shelter on the parcel of land until their house was built. Together, Ezena and Nateka stepped onto the land beneath the ceremonial canopy, situated at the front of the tent. One end was dyed the bright colors of sunrise, the other end, the rich colors of sunset, and where the two colors met in the middle laid a strip of cloth the color of bright sunshine—hope for their future.

While the procession remained at the land's boundary, the priest joined the two under the awning. With a bundle of iron spikes, they walked the perimeter of where their home was to be built. Ezena and Nateka, together, drove a spike in at each corner of the proposed edifice and the priest blessed each one.

"Take me to the entrance of this home!" the priest demanded.

Ezena and Nateka walked the priest to that area and marked it, too, with spikes. Again the priest prayed.

Nateka handed Ezena across the make-shift threshold and stood with his back to her.

"Who may enter?" the priest asked.

"None who will harm my wife or my home," Nateka shouted to the crowd. He folded his arms over his chest and shaped his expression into a fierce scowl. The onlookers cheered the completion of the ceremony.

A line of low tables, laden with platters of food, stood along an outer wall of the tent. Sheets of fabric covered the ground to shield the diners and their food from dust.

Ezena and Nateka ate together beneath the awning. Feeding each other morsels of food and sips of wine, they seemed oblivious of those around them.

Kandake watched as her friend ate from the hand of her new husband. She saw the tender care with which Nateka fed Ezena each bite.

I may be ready for this sooner than I had believed.

_51_

The morning after Ezena's marriage ceremony a runner came into Nubia. He was granted an audience with King Amani. As he entered the throne room his gaze landed upon Kandake. He dropped to the floor, prostrate, in a display of great shame and complete surrender.

"King Amani of Nubia, I bring you a message from King Zoskales of Aksum," the messenger said.

"You may rise," King Amani said.

"Please forgive my disobedience. King Zoskales assured me that if I stood in the presence of Princess Kandake, he would strip the hide from my back and turn my family out onto the Strand—none of us able to return to Aksum, ever." He extended the hand containing the message scroll out to his side. "King Zoskales requests permission to come to Nubia and offer his regret over his son's behavior and to apologize to you and the princess."

Kandake stared at the man lying on the floor.

"When would this visit be?" King Amani asked.

"He is on the Strand awaiting my return with your answer."

King Amani looked to Kandake.

I have no desire to be in the presence of anyone of that family.

Her sudden anger brought bile to her throat. Thoughts of the prince threatened to overcome her sense of reason, flooding her with a desire to cause him harm. Memory of the expression on Ezena's face throughout yesterday's ceremony exploded upon Kandake's mind. Memory of the tear-stains of Tabiry's came next.

Kandake forced herself through a calming exercise. *I will not rob my sister of what she craves.* She gave her father a sharp nod of her head.

"I will permit King Zoskales to come to Nubia," King Amani said. "He will only be allowed inside our borders with a Nubian escort." He turned aside and called for Uncle Dakká.

"Once you have refreshed yourself with food and drink, a contingent of warriors will accompany you to the Strand."

"Thank you, King Amani, ruler of Nubia." The man crawled on his belly from the throne room, never once rising from the floor or giving the offense of his back.

"What do you make of that, My King?" Kandake asked, after the messenger had left the room.

"It would appear that there is a limit to Aksum's tolerance of dishonorable behavior and Prince Gadarat may have exceeded it."

"As welcome as that thought is," Kandake said, "I find that a difficult one to believe." She walked with her father into the council chambers to wait for her uncle.

"What is it that you do not believe, Princess Kandake?" Uncle Dakká said as he entered the room.

"That the jackal, Zoskales, can be offended by his son's behavior." King Amani sipped water from the vessel in front of him.

There is no tremor in his hand, neither does his flesh sag from his bones. Your health has returned, Father.

"What does it matter, as long as his whelp remains in Aksum." He reached for the bowl of brined olives and offered them to his niece before taking one for himself.

"But he is coming to Nubia," Kandake said. "At least his father is."

Uncle Dakká turned to his brother for confirmation of what Kandake had said.

"Zoskales has requested permission to enter the kingdom," King Amani said.

"Of course you told him that he would be welcome the day horses eat elephants."

"No, I gave permission for him to enter." The king raised a hand to silence his brother's sputtering disagreement. "That is why I have called for you. I want you to escort him to Nubia with enough warriors to surround his entire party. I want your presence to assure him that I will not have my children threatened by anyone."

A slow, unpleasant smile crept across Uncle Dakká's face. "Do you know how many are in the Aksumite's party?"

"No, but I am certain his messenger can give you all of the information you need."

"Then, with your permission, My King, I will wait until tomorrow to travel—after our council meeting. A cold night's sleep upon the Strand should assist in cooling down his son's ire." He spit the olive pit into his hand. "I will go make preparations." Uncle Dakká left the room with a renewed spring in his step.

"Father," Kandake said as she watched her uncle leave. "I do not believe the Prime Warrior has any diplomatic plans in mind for his journey."

52

"You are bringing him here, My King?" Uncle Naqa asked.

"Is it not better to keep your enemies where you can see them?" Kandake asked. "We are aware of the nature of King Zoskales as well as that of his son, Prince Gadarat. Bringing them to the kingdom, under circumstances such as these, will surely rid the people of any doubt they may have had of my considering that prince as a husband."

"Yes, Princess Kandake, but he would have killed you, or at the very least caused you great harm."

"That may be, but he did not." Her eyes met those of everyone's at the table. "Our great king has planned to ensure that never happens."

"Princess Kandake is correct," King Amani said. "What I have in mind will keep Aksum from any attempt to harm Princess Kandake, or any other person of Nubia for a very long time."

He laid out his plan. The eyes of those seated at the table sparkled with amusement. Kandake settled her gaze onto her sister's. She smiled at her and gave her a nod of assurance. Tabiry giggled.

A long table had been set in the throne room. Kandake took her place, seated on the right of King Amani. Aunt Alodia and Alara stood behind them on the right. To the king's left, and one step behind him, stood Uncle Dakká and Natasen.

Kandake recalled the last time she and her father were seated in this manner. It was the day King Zoskales had come to Nubia. That meeting ended with Prince Gadarat requesting to present himself as a suitor. It was also the day her father became ill and Kandake went to bed as queen. Today things were different.

King Zoskales was not seated at the table with them as an equal. Instead, King Amani sat waiting for the Aksumite's arrival—a clear indication that her father was the one in power. King Zoskales entered the room with a Nubian escort—evidence that this was not a trusted ally. The sideways glares of Zoskales toward his son confirmed he blamed Prince Gadarat for the current circumstances.

Of the three seats offered to the Aksumites, only two were filled; one by King Zoskales and the other by his junior son, Prince Beygat. Prince Gadarat was made to stand. Kandake could not tell if the expression of pain carved into Gadarat's features was caused by the wound of his leg or the wound of his pride. Being witness to his misery set her feelings of anger to flight to be replaced by quiet satisfaction.

"You have requested this meeting," King Amani said, glaring at the man across from him. "What has Nubia to do with Aksum?"

King Zoskales winced at the words and sound of King Amani. "We of Aksum, come to ask pardon of the king of Nubia for the great offense against this kingdom brought by my son, Prince Gadarat." He squirmed in his seat. "Nubia has shared a border with Aksum for generations, enjoying a relationship that has been one of peace. That relationship has now been threatened." He glowered at the standing prince.

"In an effort to assure Nubia of Aksum's desire to continue our peaceful associations, a gift has been brought." He laid a rolled hide in the center of the table, the space between him and King Amani.

At King Amani's direction, Aunt Alodia retrieved the scroll, opened it, and read aloud. "Zoskales, the son of the great kings of Aksum, offers this gift to Nubia as a humble act of contrition, the following: a herd of goats, fifteen females and five males, one herd of cattle, thirty females, ten with calf and ten with milk, the remaining ten females not yet of age to mate and the promise of five males, yet to be born." She handed the accounting to King Amani.

"This does not begin to atone for the insult endured by Princess Kandake," King Zoskales said, "but if Nubia would allow it, Aksum will use the remaining years of my reign proving the value of my kingdom as an ally."

"And when your son rules?" King Amani leveled his eyes on Prince Gadarat. The prince had the decency to duck his head in shame.

Again Zoskales' discomfort caused him to shift in his seat. "It is with regret that I cannot speak for my son."

As if on cue, Prince Gadarat lowered himself to one knee. The move must have brought him severe pain. Beads of sweat broke out on his forehead and upper lip. "King Amani of Nubia, Princess Kandake, future queen of Nubia, I pledge, throughout my reign, that Aksum will prove to be a treasured friend to this kingdom and should it take every bow in Aksum, Nubia will flourish and stand in strength." He did not rise from his show of respect.

King Amani turned to Kandake. At her nod, he stretched out his hand to Aunt Alodia. She handed him a sheaf of hides enveloped and bound in the leather of formal decree. He returned it to her following his examination. She read aloud from it.

"As of this day, Aksum will receive from Nubia the use of this kingdom's mines of copper, and the land surrounding those mines that lie within Aksum's borders. Should Aksum's behavior, in any way, whether by political alliance or deed, appear as an act of aggression against the kingdom of Nubia, now or in the future, it will be interpreted as an act of war and these lands will revert to the sole property of Nubia."

She placed the treatise on the table before King Zoskales to place his official seal. With that completed, Prince Gadarat arose from the floor.

"Thank you for your generosity, King Amani," Zoskales said. "With your permission, we will return to Aksum."

"Prince Dakká will ensure that you arrive to the Strand in safety."

King Zoskales grimaced, a clear indication of his awareness that the insult to Nubia had not yet been forgiven.

_53_

Kandake sat at evening meal with her family. Surrounded by aunts, uncles, and cousins, she was reminded of the true wealth of her family—love and relationship. Great Mother laughed at some antic by one of Aunt Alodia's youngest children. Her father allowed her mother to fuss over him without complaint. Her uncles Dakká and Naqa enjoyed their usual teasing banter about Uncle Naqa's wardrobe, garments painted to match the landscape of the kingdom. She leaned back from the table, satisfied more by the company than the food.

"Father, I have something important to tell you," Tabiry said. "I have chosen!"

"You have? Which of your suitors is it to be?" he asked, munching upon a radish his wife popped into his mouth.

"Shen, the warrior of Scythia!"

Silence fell upon the room like a flood over a flame. Not a soul stirred. The beating of a bee's wings would have seemed deafening in the quiet.

"Shen is to become my brother?" Kandake asked, grinning at her sister and whooping in delight. "A definite promise of more strong children in Nubia!"

Stephanie Jefferson loves all forms of story – oral, written, cinematic and any other form you can think of. She says she writes because of the way it makes her brain feel. Her greatest desire is to craft a story the reader never wants to end.

Stephanie lives in Prescott Valley, AZ with her husband and gets bossed around by her 17-pound cairn terrier, Mr. Jenkins.

Visit her website www.stephaniejefferson.com